The Missing Episodes

DOCTOR WHO
THE NIGHTMARE FAIR

based on the BBC television series from the untelevised script by
Graham Williams by arrangement with BBC Books, a division of
BBC Enterprises Ltd

GRAHAM WILLIAMS

TARGET

A TARGET BOOK
published by
the Paperback Division of
W. H. ALLEN & Co. Plc

A Target Book
Published in 1989
By the Paperback Division of
W. H. Allen & Co. Plc
Sekforde House, 175/9 St. John Street,
London, EC1V 4LL

Printed and bound in Great Britain by
Cox & Wyman Ltd, Reading

ISBN 0 426 20334 8

Chapter One

The scream was choked off halfway through, to be followed by hoarse, panting gasps. A dull crash and a scuffle came one after the other and then there was silence.

Nothing moved. Nothing visible. The shadow of a cloud passing the moon dulled the scene for a moment, but when the shadow had gone, nothing had changed. The tarmac stretched, glistening in the recent rain, the wooden walls of the building loomed up into the black night sky and the dull, dirty windows grinned down like empty eye sockets . . .

The scream started again, then changed abruptly to a grunting sound, panting, rasping with exertion. The wooden door smashed back on its hinges as a man crashed out and fell to the ground. He lay for a moment, stunned or exhausted, then half-shook his head and turned to look back into the building. Through the open door could be seen a glow – a softly, gently pulsating glow, the red colour burning and tearing at the edges as though testifying to the tremendous power of whatever was the source of the light, a dull, aching red light . . .

The man's face contorted in terror as the glow deepened, brightened, deepened, brightened . . . He made as though to rise and he started to scream again, a low, broken wail as he realised his leg was trapped by whatever was inside the building. The wail took on a desperate, despairing edge as he felt himself being dragged back, back, until, as his last broken attempts to hang on to the door frame proved useless, the cry rose to a pitch of absolute terror and he disappeared from view. The red light rose to a new intensity and locked, the pulsing frozen as the scream was cut off as though by a knife.

The silence was complete and the red light faded slowly, gently, away, returning the scene to the black of the night and the empty, scudding clouds across the moon . . .

'Perfect!' cried the Doctor, in the voice he normally reserved for a superbly delivered inside seamer or a Gamellean sunset. 'There's nowhere else like it in the Universe. Not *this* Universe, anyway . . .' He held a brass telescope to his eye, and moved it slowly across the horizon. The breeze ruffled his hair and beside him Peri shivered and pushed her hands further into her anorak pockets.

'They're trying to build one on the rim of the Crab Nebula,' he continued, 'but the design concept's all wrong. They're trying to build it for a *purpose* . . .'

'What's wrong with that?' asked Peri.

'Everything! You can't build a place like this for a mere *purpose*!' He snapped the telescope shut and spun to face her. 'And don't talk to me of "fluid lines provoked by the ergonomic imperatives . . ." '

'All right then, I won't,' murmured Peri, as though the comment had been on the tip of her tongue.

'Or the strict adherence to the symbolic form, the classical use of conceptual space . . .' He flung his arm dramatically to one side, as if he thought he was back in the Roman Forum and poor old Julius was waiting for a decent send-off. 'Designers' gobbledeygook,' he denounced, gravely. 'Architects' flim-flam,' he added, in agreement with himself. 'The tired consensus of a jaded age,' he concluded, finally burying the conversation.

6

'I entirely agree,' said Peri, trying to be helpful without the faintest idea as to what particular bee was buzzing around in the Doctor's bonnet just now.

'No, you'll never win that argument here,' added the Doctor, both smugly and unnecessarily. 'This is absolute, perfect, classic *frivolity*.'

Peri followed his gaze three hundred feet down to the sight of Blackpool, spread before them like a toy town, the trams clattering along the promenade towards the funfair in the middle distance.

'It's OK, I suppose,' she shrugged. 'If you like that sort of thing . . .'

'*OK*?' the Doctor whirled to face her, his face a mask of fury. '*OK*?' Words, unlikely though it seems, failed him. 'I'll show you OK,' he muttered through clenched teeth as he grabbed her hand and pulled her, protesting, across the observation platform of Blackpool Tower towards the waiting lifts.

'Where are we going?' wailed Peri, fearful that at last she'd pushed the Time Lord over the edge and he was dragging her towards some dreadful punishment known only to the near-eternal. He stopped so hard she bumped into him. He pushed his face to within millimetres of hers and snarled gratingly, 'You're going to enjoy yourself if it kills you!' And with that he carried on to the lifts, with Peri forced to go with him or part company with an arm she was quite attached to . . .

The young man, for the hundredth time, let his gaze wander up from the bare table where he was seated to the simple clock on the wall. Two whole minutes since the last time he'd looked. His gaze carried on, over the grey plain walls, the neon striplight, the plain chair in the corner. He'd been in Police interview rooms before, several of them, and he couldn't tell one from the other. Perhaps that was the idea. He didn't have much time for your average criminal, and, truth to tell, didn't have much time for your average copper either. And as for your average Police Station . . . He'd never had much to do with any of them, not until the last few months anyway, and he was too young and too bright to try and unravel the thinking that went behind the design of anything to do with authority.

At last he was distracted by heavy footsteps outside in the corridor, footsteps which came to a shuffling halt outside his door. The door opened to reveal the moon-faced but not unkind constable who had been humouring him for the best part of the morning. The constable held the door open for a thick-set man in his late forties, dressed in what seemed to be a perfectly cut three-piece suit, a man whom the constable treated as though he were second cousin to the Lord High Executioner.

'Mr Kevin Stoney?' asked the suited man, politely. Kevin nodded without replying. The man hefted the thick file in his hand as he sat in the chair opposite.

'Didn't take much finding, did this, lad. Right on top of the pile. You're quite a regular visitor to our humble abode, aren't you?'

'Not by choice,' muttered Kevin.

'Well they all say that, lad,' observed the man with a small chuckle. 'I'm surprised we haven't met before.'

'I've asked often enough,' observed Kevin.

'Aye. "Someone in authority", I believe you stipulated,' added the man, referring to the top page of the file.

'That's right,' affirmed Kevin stoutly.

'Well, will I do? I mean, I'm only a lowly Inspector, but we could try the Chief Inspector, or Superintendent, or the Chief Superintendent –'

'You'll do,' nodded Kevin.

8

'You sure? Chief Constable's not got much on today, shall I –'

'No that's all right,' replied Kevin, not wanting to rise to the bait.

The Inspector looked at him thoughtfully for a moment, lips pursed, then, with a small nod, he decided to get down to business.

'This statement of yours, referring to the events of last night . . .' He tapped the statement in the file with a solid-looking forefinger. 'Truthful statement, is it?'

'Yes.'

'Just a simple statement of the facts . . .'

'That's right.' The reply sounded more defensive than he had intended. The Inspector took the statement and held it carefully, as though it was fragile – or dangerous – and read slowly and carefully from it.

' "The figure was glowing red, with some green or blue at the edges . . . about seven feet tall and heavily built . . . the red colour seemed to pulsate, giving the impression that the figure was increasing then decreasing in size. It had no eyes, no ears, nothing I could describe as a face . . ." Incredible –'

'I saw it –' started Kevin, gritting his teeth.

'No, no,' protested the Inspector. 'What's incredible is that at this point the sergeant who took your statement failed to determine whether there were any distinguishing marks on this . . . person . . .'

The moon-faced constable attempted, without success, to stifle a chuckle at this. The Inspector turned slowly towards him.

'This is no laughing matter, lad. One more outburst like that and I'll have you out in that amusement park every night till dawn from now until your retirement party.'

The constable, for a split second, didn't know if this was another example of the Inspector's wit. Wisely, he

9

decided it wasn't, and straightened to attention. The Inspector turned back to Kevin.

'As I was saying, it was a definite oversight on our part, but I'm sure you'll agree we shouldn't have much trouble picking chummy out in the shopping centre, should we?'

'Not even your lot, no,' agreed Kevin. 'But it was the amusement park, not the shopping centre.'

'Even there, lad,' continued the Inspector, nodding confidently, 'reckon we'd spot him, in time. Mind you, some of the types who hang round those pinball machines – we might have to form a line-up at that . . .'

Kevin decided to let it ride. The Inspector continued leafing through the file, going a little further back.

'"The figure of a Chinese Mandarin, appearing and disappearing into thin air . . ."' He turned more pages. '"Strange lights appeared about twenty feet off the ground . . ."' Yet more pages. '"Strange lights appeared at *ground level* . . ."' He closed the file and placed it carefully on the table. 'So there was nothing unusual about last night then?'

Kevin returned the calm, level stare, still refusing to rise to the jibe.

'I mean, it seems to me it were just like any other night you – er – "find yourself"' in the park, eh?'

'Last night the Mandarin wasn't there.'

'No Mandarin,' repeated the Inspector, heavily. He leant forward, elbows on the table. 'Right, lad. You tell me all about this Mandarin . . .'

The Mandarin swept in through the door almost regally, the tall figure erect, walking in long, gracious strides. The door closed obediently behind him with the softest of clicks. He crossed immediately to sit behind the huge carved desk in a huge carved chair. He paused for a moment, still but intensely alert.

The room seemed to fit around him like a glove – high ceilings and walls, panelled in English wood though decorated in the Oriental style of the nineteenth century: heavy brocaded drapes, rich, ponderous carvings, subdued, almost gloomy lights which allowed the brilliant colours of the paintings and tapestries to stand out with three-dimensional effect.

His gaze slowly turned to a large crystal ball, mounted on a round mahogany base before him. He reached his hand out slowly, delicately, and, with the lightest touch of his fingers, began to rotate it. As he did so, the picture on the large viewing screen set into the wall opposite swirled as though filled with smoke, then began to swim and clear as the fingers moved and sought their target.

Within moments a recognisable picture emerged. As if from a very great height, the Blackpool funfair could be seen, waiting in the weak spring sunshine. The fingers and the picture moved again and the funfair moved closer and closer, the images growing and passing as the seeing-eye moved down amongst the arcades, the rides and the crowds, coming to rest on the unmistakable figure of the Doctor.

The Mandarin removed his hand from the crystal ball with the same deliberate delicacy with which he had placed it there, and he settled back in his chair to view the scene, the hint of a cold smile crossing his aristocratic face . . .

The Doctor regarded the giant pink-coloured growth he was holding with more than usual suspicion.

'Edible?' he asked. 'You can't be serious.'

'Sure it is,' Peri maintained.

'They didn't have this at Brighton.'

'It wasn't invented then. I thought you knew all about Earth History.'

11

'All the salient facts, yes.'

'Well, one thing I've never heard candy floss called is salient,' admitted Peri.

'Candy floss,' repeated the Doctor.

'Go on, try it.'

Mastering his automatic distrust of sugar-based pink growths, borne of the experience on a thousand worlds where such growths are the most merciless of the inhabitants, the Doctor took a small nibble. And then another. And another.

'Astonishing,' he remarked as he grappled with a long frond. 'The triumph of volume over mass taken to its logical conclusion . . . Where did you say you found it?'

'In the booth over there –'

'No, no. The five-pound note you used to pay for it.'

'The TARDIS cloakroom. In a sporran. At least it looked like a sporran. I nearly brought that too, but it wouldn't have gone with this outfit.'

'Good Heavens! It must be Jamie's. And I'd always thought him so . . . careful with his cash . . .'

'He won't mind, will he?'

'I'm sure he did – will – does – Oh, I don't know. This *is* an emergency, isn't it?'

He beamed around at his fellow holiday-makers for confirmation. The only response he received was from a very dour man in an enormous padded anorak, who gestured rudely that he should move along with the queue.

'Are you sure this is what you want?' asked Peri.

'More sure now than I was,' replied the Doctor, taking another nibble from the candy floss.

'I mean *this*,' retorted Peri, gesturing at the towering frame of the giant rollercoaster which craned over their heads.

12

'I'll say,' enthused the Doctor. 'I've been looking back to this for years.'

'Couldn't we have gone to Hawaii?' moaned Peri, shivering again. 'Miles of sand, waving palms, beautiful, beautiful sunshine –'

'Poppycock,' snorted the Doctor. 'I'll never understand you lot – a long bath in cold sodium chloride solution, then wallowing about on a bed of mica crystals whilst undergoing severe exposure to hard ultra-violet bombardment. If you ask me your summer holidays go a long way towards accounting for the basic irrationality of the human race . . .'

'Next you'll be telling me you *planned* on coming here.'

'If it had been my plan, it would have been a jolly good one.'

'Your attitude towards self-determination could be called pragmatic . . .'

'You mean there's another sort of self-determination? It was a malfunction, that's all.'

'That's all? We get yanked halfway across the Milky Way inside a couple of nano-seconds and that's all?'

'You're very hard to please, Peri . . .'

'I feel as though my stomach's still the other side of Alpha Centauri . . .'

'So it is, I suppose, if you take the Old Castellan's last stab at Universal Relativity slightly out of context . . . Don't you like it, even a little bit?'

The Doctor seemed genuinely hurt that Peri shouldn't share his enthusiasm for the Great British Wet Spring, which leads with such comforting predictability to the Great British Wet Summer, and Peri felt she should soften the blow.

'I do, I do. It's just not the centre of the Universe, is it?'

13

The Doctor looked around, as if to get his bearings. 'Well,' he muttered, after a moment, 'it's close . . .'

'A space-time vortex, you said . . .'

'Yes,' he affirmed, nodding vigorously.

'So strong it could only be at the centre of the Danger Zone, you said . . .'

'It had all the appearances –' he agreed, nodding fiercely now.

'The Nexus of the Primeval Cauldron of Space-Time itself were the exact words you used . . .'

'That's a very apt turn of phrase!' he exclaimed, imbued once again with enthusiasm for his own eloquence.

'For *this*!' squawked Peri, flinging out her arm in what the Doctor later considered to be an over-dramatic gesture but which nevertheless took in the full scale and majesty of Blackpool's outdoor amusement park. The Doctor nibbled his candy floss again, rather sheepishly this time.

'Perhaps just a little florid,' he murmured, as the line moved forward again towards the entrance to the rollercoaster.

Kevin flinched instinctively as the Inspector leaned forward to emphasise his next point.

'. . . and my colleagues in the Uniformed Branch tell me they've organised better than a dozen additional foot patrols over the past three months on the basis of your . . . information.' He stabbed the air with his forefinger and then seemed to pull himself back. 'Now, that's a helluva lot of extra Police time, and they found precisely . . . nothing.'

'There was nothing going on the nights those coppers were out,' protested Kevin, rather unnecessarily.

'Nothing at all,' agreed the Inspector. 'No flashing lights, no Mandarins, no jolly red giants. What d'you

14

reckon they do? Snap their fingers and disappear the minute they see our boys, or look into a crystal ball and see us coming before we know ourselves?'

Kevin was about to guess which one, but the Inspector stopped him with a very hard look.

'You were warned off making any more reports of sighting your brother at that fair. We are not a missing persons bureau. Your brother is over sixteen years of age and has committed no crime of which we are aware –'

Again Kevin was about to protest, but the Inspector ploughed on like a battleship in heavy seas.

'You will stop wasting Police time, you will stop reporting flashing lights, Chinese Mandarins, little green men from Mars or great big red ones from anywhere else and if you find yourself even close to that amusement park one more time, I shall take it very personally indeed. So personally I will more than likely lose what remains of my professional detachment and throw the flaming book at you. Do I make myself clear?'

This last was delivered with such a force as to leave no need for clarification whatsoever. Kevin swallowed and rose from his chair. 'Can I go now?'

Truscott sighed and leaned back heavily. 'Aye, you can go. I hope you find your brother, son, I really do. And when you do find him, that's the next and last time I want to see you. All right?'

Kevin, reluctantly, could see that the policeman was not half as hard as he made himself out, and he nodded, tired. 'Aye, all right.' He turned to make towards the door. Truscott stopped him.

'But, lad,' he offered, in a conversational tone of voice, 'you spot any more of them Red Giants, you send them along to Preston North End. They could do with all the help they can get . . .'

This time he did not rebuke the constable's chortle, and Kevin angrily left to make his own way out, wondering which section of the Inspector's book was going to hit him first.

The blue lacquered fingernail, at least two inches longer than the parent finger, extended like a shiny fossilised snake to press an ivory button set into the desk. With a whisper, a door across the room swung open smoothly, revealing a well built man, bearded and dressed all in black, who strode purposefully towards the Mandarin. He stopped in front of the desk and bowed with practised ease from the waist, awaiting a barely perceptible gesture from the fingernail before speaking.

'My Lord, the spacecraft is like no other we have seen.' The voice was gravelly, dragged reluctantly from the depths of a broad chest, coloured with an accent definitely not British, but round and rich with much travelling. 'In truth, it seems hardly a spacecraft at all, but there is nothing else at the co-ordinates you gave us. I could detect no propulsion units, no aerofoils, no means of access. I have set the barrier around it, as you instructed. Of the occupants, there is no sign . . .'

'We have them, Stefan,' assured the Mandarin softly. 'The bio-data will confirm his identity beyond any shadow of a doubt.'

The elegant hand moved once more to the crystal ball and the picture on the viewing screen swam into focus, the Doctor's face filling it corner to corner. Not one of the Doctor's best poses, it must be said; he was beaming tightly and manically, his eyes wide with anticipation and blinking quickly. The observing lens obeyed the Mandarin's fingers as they made tiny, delicate movements, moving down the Doctor's face, down his neck, across the shoulder and down the arm, to steady on the hands, which were gripping a safety

16

bar tightly. The Mandarin's fingers moved again on the crystal ball and the part of the picture featuring the Doctor's hands started to turn negative, black fingers and black nails gripping a now white bar. The Mandarin leaned forward slightly and spoke in a soft but penetrating whisper.

'Doctor . . .'

'Yes?' responded the Doctor.

'Yes what?' asked Peri.

'You called me.'

'Called you? I'm sitting right next to you.'

'Excellent.'

Peri looked at him with more than usual puzzlement. Perhaps the strain of this particular stretch of his second, or third, or one-hundred-and-third childhood was getting to him. It was really very difficult coping with a supposedly mature man of *very* indeterminate age whose natural behaviour mimicked a seven-year-old more often than a seven-hundred-year-old. The train of thought, familiar and unproductive though it was, broke as the car gave a sharp jerk forward.

'Aaagh,' gurgled the Doctor in an ecstasy of anticipation. The rollercoaster ride settled into its smooth, noisy glide away from the platform and the first car immediately began the steep climb towards the sky. Peri settled into a taut, rigid posture as she prepared for the worst. The Doctor had not moved a muscle for the last five minutes, except to refer to a non-existent conversation, but the transfixed posture he had adopted as soon as he'd sat in the car was now, if anything, more pronounced. Perhaps it was something to do with the eyes . . . the wild, staring eyes . . .

A groan, starting somewhere near her navel, grew to a full size screech as the car reached its apogee and Peri saw for the first time the scale of the drop before them.

17

From here she could see the whole amusement park, the promenade, the electric trams trundling along and the cold sea stretching away past the famous Tower towards the far horizon.

At least, she would have seen them easily had she not slammed her eyes shut in the same split second as she saw the rails running down, suicide fashion, in the near-vertical descent.

As the car plummeted earthwards, the screech became a wail became a scream as it floated out far behind them, lost in a moment under the thundering wheels . . .

Chapter Two

Footsteps echoed mournfully down the empty, dimly lit corridor. Here and there the high-tech alloy construction gave way to bare rock, glistening wetly in the half-light as the corridor stretched away into the distance, with branches and junctions all but hidden in the gloom. The footsteps were halting, dragging, evidence of a limp before their owner even appeared around a corner, making his way slowly towards the airlock style door which terminated the corridor.

The owner of the footsteps looked older than just the years could make him, a heavy exhaustion seeming to make every step more painful than the limp could account for, the shoulder-length grey hair acting as a weight his neck could hardly bear, the deep, long lines in his face looking more like surgical scars than the product of time. He carried, with both hands, a small earthenware pitcher and perhaps it weighed a ton and perhaps it just seemed that way.

Set into the alloy wall of the corridor was an incongruous wood and iron door, standing shut on stout metal strap hinges. A window near the top of the door, covered with thick iron bars, gave viewing access to the room within. The old man stopped and made to open the door when the airlock sprang open with an almost silent 'whoosh' and Stefan stepped through. The old man averted his eyes and reached for the handle to the old wooden door.

'Shardlow,' snapped Stefan. The old man started as though the handle of the door was connected to the electricity supply. He froze. Stefan approached him. The old man seemed rigid with fear. As Stefan stopped by him, he spoke more softly, but in a somehow more threatening way.

'Shouldn't you be looking after dinner, Shardlow?'

'I was just preparing the guest room, sir,' replied Shardlow, in a quiet voice, full of fear.

'We do have other guests, Shardlow. I imagine they're getting hungry . . .'

'Yes, sir,' Shardlow half-bowed abjectly and turned from the wooden door towards the airlock. Not quickly enough for Stefan, apparently, for he called, with a whipping edge to his voice:

'And hurry, man! You know how jealous our Lord is of his reputation for hospitality!'

'Yes, sir. Immediately, sir,' and, pathetically, the old man tried to hurry his pace as much as he could, water from the pitcher slopping onto his coarse linen trousers and splashing onto the floor. Stefan laughed, or at least that's how *he* would have described it. To the old man it was a vicious, evil cackle which he had known, for more time than seemed possible, to be a prelude to pain, or hunger, or humiliation, depending on the mood of the saturnine demon who called himself Stefan . . .

Kevin thrust his hands deeper into the pockets of his windcheater as he hurried through the gigantic wooden arch which acted as the entrance to the amusement park. The place was hardly crowded at this time of year, unlike the high summer months when you could hardly move through the main concourse, and trying to get into any of the rides or booths was more a question of stamina and brute strength than anything else. A good half of the attractions were still boarded up from the winter break, and the litter swept along by the chilly breeze gave a greater feeling of desolation to the place than was strictly warranted. In all, a couple of dozen people were out strolling, most of them well wrapped up, a few rather determinedly eating toffee apples or even candy floss in what struck Kevin as defiant a gesture as he was making himself by simply being there. The warning from Inspector Truscott was still fresh in his mind as he hurried past the ghost train, which was just opening, and past the uniformed police constable chatting to the bored young lady in the ticket kiosk. Kevin had the sense not to pull the collar of the windcheater up around his ears, but it took a conscious effort to beat the instinct all the same.

Instead, he increased his pace and took on a more determined stride as he made towards the spot he had visited the previous night, an almost derelict eyesore patch of tarmac behind the video-game arcade, under the towering shadow of the rollercoaster.

Shardlow's eyes closed in silent relief as he rounded the corner and saw that Stefan was nowhere to be seen. The Mandarin's lieutenant must have better things – well anyway more urgent things – to do, thought the old man, with a murmured prayer of thanks to a deity whose name he had forgotten. Often it would be Stefan's idea of fun to join Shardlow in serving dinner, making barbs, taunts and threats which invariably left the old man a quivering wreck at the end of the experience.

He hefted the heavy pail he was carrying into the other hand and moved towards the first of the doors in the corridor. This too was wooden with a barred window in the top third and, like its companions which lined the sides of this corridor, it also had a metal flap set near the bottom, about a foot across and half as high. Below the flap and at right angles to it, was a metal shelf of about the same size. Shardlow dipped his hand into the bucket he was carrying and pulled out a reeking gobbet of bloody, raw meat, which he carefully placed on the shelf. He tried to take no notice of the hurrying, scuttling noise from behind the door. Carefully, he moved to the side of the door and pulled the peg holding the flap shut out of its retaining hasp. Gingerly he opened the flap upwards, still taking care to keep clear as he did so.

A giant blue-black claw which could only just move through the opening appeared and with a delicate but horrible finality the serrated, razor-sharp edges closed around the meat and drew it inside.

Shardlow waited patiently for a moment, ignoring now the slobbering, tearing sounds from behind the door, then he closed the flap gently, locked it with the peg, and moved on with his pail to the next door.

Nothing, thought Kevin, glumly. An absolute, total, magnificent unbroken record. Zilch. He had come inside the arcade to warm up a bit, his examination of the area outside having proved as fruitless as he thought it would. Why he'd bothered, he didn't know. The spot where he'd heard the screams and come running and seen the receding light was as bare as you'd expect a bare patch of tarmac behind a video arcade to be. Bare.

He looked around, almost curling his lip, settling eventually for a sniff at the dozens of machines crowded into the arcade. Everything, ranging from the original Space Invaders and one-armed bandits to the latest products of the fertile brains of half the best universities in the western hemisphere, was locked into the latest way of whamming and bamming and shooting 'em down. He'd never been able to understand why Geoff had been besotted with them ever since he was tall enough to reach up and feed the coins into the slot. Not that the boy wasn't good . . . quite the reverse, the

22

boy was terrific. He hadn't been called the VideoKid for nothing. Well, everyone's got to be good at *something*.

The idle thought was interrupted as a small, middle-aged woman in a thick, and by the looks of it old, brown coat, bumped into him.

'Sorry, hen,' the woman muttered in a Glasgow accent, absently though, as she looked around with obvious concern, this way and that, trying to see around and over the machines blocking her view.

'You havenae seen my – ah, you wouldn't know, would you –' Distracted she carried on her way, with neither Kevin nor anyone else any the wiser as to who or what she was looking for. This issue at least was settled as she called out, very tentatively at first, then more urgently, 'Tyrone . . . ? Are y'there, Tyrone? Tyrone . . . ?'

Tyrone remained unmoved and unmoving as one of the men in the white coats moved away from his side, having fixed another contact disc with electrical wires dangling from it to a spot slightly off-centre on his bare abdomen. Discs were already in place on both his wrists, his forearms, his chest and at two places on his forehead. His unseeing eyes stared straight ahead as another man approached with an opthalmoscope and used it to examine first the eye, and then the blood vessels behind . . .

The noise from the video arcade could barely be heard as yet another man reached into the kidney dish on a trolley by the examination table and began to prepare a waiting hypodermic syrette . . .

The deceleration of the car threw the Doctor and Peri heavily against the safety bar in front of them. At least, it did Peri. The Doctor seemed to be cast in pre-stressed

23

concrete, with the obvious exception of the mop of hair, looking as though it had been prepared for a long night at the disco with an inferior brand of gel.

The car drew level to the platform they had left several aeons ago and came to a surprisingly gentle stop. The other passengers, laughing, giggling or looking a paler shade of green dismounted and made their way to the exit. Peri brushed back her hair.

'Phew! That was fun! That was really fun! I'm amazed, I didn't expect to like it one little bit –'

By now she couldn't help noticing that the Doctor had been struck immobile, arms straight out in front, still riveted to the safety bar, eyes wide open, staring manically ahead, mouth firmly shut, teeth clamped together as if with superglue, the whole face set in a frantic, ecstatic beam normally seen only on the visages of winners on a television quiz show.

'Doctor? Doctor?' She placed a hand on his arm. The only response from him was a strangled gargle of a noise. 'Doctor?' she repeated, anxiously now. 'Are you all right?'

There was another of the strained, awful strangling noises, but at least this time the eyes moved, jerkily and only slightly, but they moved. Peri shook his arm gently. The trance, at last, broke. He took in a great breath, a giant breath and finally got the words out.

'I have never, not ever, not in any of my lives . . . I left at least one of my hearts at the bottom of that last dip – or it might still be at the top of the one before – I have shot through Black Holes, I have sailed through Supernovae, I have eaten Vanarian Sun Seed Cake, but I have never, never, never, never . . .' He shook his head, unbelieving, and, had Peri not known him better, she would have sworn he was at a loss for words.

'I really enjoyed it,' she announced again, happily.

24

'Enjoyed it? *Enjoyed* it?' He nearly exploded with indignation at the paucity of such a reaction. 'It was . . . MAGNIFICENT . . .'

'Shall we go round again?' asked Peri, in what could pass for an innocent sort of voice.

The Doctor looked at her wildly for a moment, the monumental scale of the suggestion taking him by surprise. 'Again? Yes, yes . . . again . . .' The wisdom of the ages came, unbidden to his rescue. 'In a while we will, yes.' And with that he nodded vigorously and started to climb out of the car.

As suddenly as it had started, the chattering of the high-speed printer ceased. Stefan carefully tore off the printed sheet and made his way towards the Mandarin, who was standing, listening attentively to a technician in a white coat who looked distinctly as though he had the better right to the eastern style wardrobe the Mandarin favoured.

Indeed, of the eight or ten technicians in the room, over half were Oriental in origin: Japanese, or Taiwanese, or Korean, it would be hard for the uneducated western eye to tell. They stood or sat or studied against banks of the most sophisticated electronic equipment currently available, and against some which would not yet be available to the public, or industry, or the government, for generations.

Tall cabinets of mainframe computers, squat cabinets of data-analysers, wide cabinets of surveillance monitors, stood in ranks around and across the brightly lit room, needles twitching, lights flashing, digital counters whirring up and down as if giving the cue to the white-coated men in silent dedication, unceasing industry, implacable purpose . . .

Stefan handed the short sheet of paper to the Mandarin, effecting another of his small, deferential bows as he did so. The Mandarin studied the paper for a moment and a smile broke the hard line of his mouth. Stefan could contain his puzzlement no longer.

'*Two* hearts, Lord?' he asked. 'Perhaps the equipment . . .' He looked around the room, unwilling, even unable to suggest that the busy silent monsters which surrounded him could be at fault.

'If there were only one, Stefan, then I should be sadly disappointed.' He turned to one of the technicians with whom he had been talking. 'Match them now, please, Soonking. DNA and RNA profiles.'

The technician adjusted the controls on one of the banks of equipment and monitored its progress closely on a VDU. Around him the machines switched to a different pattern of activity as they moved together on a joint purpose. The left-hand side of the screen filled with the familiar double-helix pattern, over which another gradually took shape. The two moved together and merged into one. The right-hand side of the screen was filled with dozens of multi-digit numbers, whirring up and down faster than could be registered. Eventually they too slowed and came to an agreement.

'A little older, probably no wiser, but certainly the same Time Lord,' pronounced the Mandarin, the thin smile becoming more contented, more final. 'It's good to see you again,' he leaned forward slightly as he breathed in the same deep whisper as before, 'Doctor . . .'

'Yes?' asked the Doctor.
  'Yes what?' replied Peri.
  'You did it again!' protested the Doctor.
  'Did what?'
  'Called my name.'
  'I did no such thing!'

26

A rip-snorter of an argument could have started between them there and then, but the Doctor spun his head round to another direction as he heard the call again. He searched through what passed for the crowd outside the entrance to the rollercoaster ride, looking for the person who was so obviously trying to engage his attention. The direction kept changing, though, and for several moments he was confused and disorientated, swinging this way and that. To anyone not privy to his private call-line, such as Peri, his behaviour was odd even by his own highly individual standards.

'What?' he asked out loud, to no one in particular, 'Who is it? Who's there?'

'Are you all right?' asked Peri, more because she thought someone should than in the hope of any positive answer. The Doctor was very obviously not all right at all. He spun round again, to face yet another direction. 'Perhaps that ride shook you up?' she asked, hopefully.

'It's a man's voice,' he announced with surprise and something approaching pleasure, as though the question of gender had been plaguing him for most of his life. 'Stupid of me, but it's clearer now.'

'What man?' asked Peri doubtfully, looking around at dozens of men in view, walking through the thin Springtime sunshine. But the Doctor either didn't hear her, or didn't know, for he was off and walking quickly as he cocked his head this way and that, trying to follow the Sirens' call that only he could hear.

Peri had no option but to follow him, which became more difficult than it seemed as his pace quickened. They half-walked, half-ran up the main concourse, past the dodgem ride, past the ghost train, past all the hoopla stalls and the hall of mirrors, the ever-laughing wooden drunken sailor swaying and cackling as they passed in such a positive and nasty fashion that Peri did a double-take at him – it was as if the sailor knew something they

27

didn't . . . Until at last, the Doctor's pace slowed and he looked with anticipation tinged with suspicion at the low profile ahead of the video arcade . . .

'He was right by me!' protested the Scotswoman. 'I just went up to get some change from yon Jimmy up there.' She gestured rather wildly in the direction of a surly youth in the change booth, who looked distinctly uncomfortable at the thought of any attention whatsoever coming his way. 'And then when I turned round, he'd just gone!'

Kevin had by now managed to edge his way unobtrusively closer to the woman, through the small knot of people who had gathered. If the story wasn't the same as his own, it at least involved a boy who had gone missing in very close proximity to an area which he knew had more than one secret to hide.

'Look, love,' replied the manager in a heavy Liverpudlian accent, 'we get all kindsa kids in 'ere. If they're under sixteen and unaccompanied, out they go.' Kevin looked sceptically at the half-dozen or so kids under sixteen in the arcade at that moment, and saw no rush of adults to claim them. 'He could have said he was with his ma, couldn't he?' continued the manager in his thin whine.

'He wouldnae just go wanderin',' announced the woman positively. 'He's daft, but he's no' that daft.'

The Doctor apologised to Kevin as he bumped into him, edging closer to the woman and the manager. 'There's something wrong here,' he muttered to Peri in a fierce whisper. Kevin's face registered interest at the remark made immediately behind him.

'That poor lady's lost her child, that's what's wrong,' protested Peri vehemently.

'No, something else,' insisted the Doctor, 'the whole place . . . the whole feel of it . . .'

The Doctor certainly had Kevin's undivided attention.

'Are you turning psychic or something?' asked Peri, with approaching alarm. She didn't want to cope with the problems of a fifth dimension. She'd not really got used to the idea of a fourth.

'Psychic?' the Doctor was taken aback. 'You don't turn psychic. You either are or you aren't. Unfortunately, I aren't, not much anyway,' he finished, matter-of-factly.

The metaphysical dimension of the conversation was brought to an abrupt end by the piercing shriek of the Scottish woman, who pushed her way through the crowd towards the pasty-faced youth standing, or rather swaying, at the entrance to the arcade.

'Tyrone! Where have you been? I've been goin' nearly mental!'

Tyrone couldn't, or wouldn't, reply. He just shook his head slightly and had about him the distinct air of one who knows that in the very near future he's going to be violently and most thoroughly sick. Mum had leapt to the same conclusion, familiar as she undoubtedly was with her pale offspring.

'It's all them toffee apples,' she howled. 'That an' all them fizzy drinks . . . and this place . . .' She glared again at the manager, who shrugged as he must have shrugged a couple of million times before.

'Come on, son, let's get ye home. Och, yer dad's goin' tae be that mad.' This last seemed little to improve Tyrone's condition, and with a last baleful glare at the manager the woman ushered her son outside, presumably back to the vengeful clans mustering even now.

'Well that's all right, then,' pronounced Peri, happily certain that all was well with the world. The Doctor seemed to be of an entirely different opinion, for he was not listening, not to Peri at any rate. Again he was turning his head, this way and that. And again Peri was both concerned and exasperated. Kevin, on the other hand, seemed even more interested than before and as unobtrusively as he could, watched the Doctor intently.

The Doctor swung on Peri sharply. 'You didn't hear that?' he demanded, a very direct question, as though he was conducting an experiment in a laboratory.

'Hear what?' asked Peri, helplessly.

'Someone calling my name.'

'No, nothing.'

'Right, not a loudspeaker then,' he announced with quiet satisfaction. 'A psi broadcast?' he asked, in a reasonable tone of voice, and answered himself just as reasonably, 'No, impossibly narrow band . . . Old-fashioned telepathy then. But so clear, so direct, so . . . expert –' He might have continued this quite antisocial one-way conversation for hours had not he heard the voice again, for he was off at speed, calling out to Peri as he swept off. 'Come on!'

She had little choice but to follow him, and Kevin, who had all the choice in the world, hurried out after both of them.

If it had not been for the sense of purpose and the positive directions he was taking, the Doctor's dogged following of the audio scent would have looked distinctly odd. As it was, it looked only slightly odd. Again, he veered this way and that as he picked up a stronger whiff from one direction than another, sometimes spinning around to take a different tack altogether, stopping to verify a change of direction before pursuing it with even more vigour than before. By now the suspicious look on his face had deepened and passed, as he became more and more sure that he was being led. For the moment, until this particular mystery was solved, he was happy to fall in with whoever was directing his movements. The simple conundrum of how this effect was being achieved was enough to keep him reasonably interested. He had time to reflect, however, that if it went on for much longer he would become extremely irritated, which, as the whole Universe would witness, was wholly foreign to his even-tempered nature . . .

Peri was already irritated enough. Following the Doctor was, after all, more a way of life than a mere physical proximity, but this particular gadfly journey was making her dizzy. She stopped herself several times from calling out to him. What, after all, would she say? Not, 'Stop'. Not 'What are you doing?' She'd tried them all, and they none of them worked, not at times like this.

Kevin was following them both as he might have followed expert archaeologists if he were looking for a city he had lost. These two were the first characters he'd come across in months who behaved even more oddly than he did in the funfair. They were on to something, or they were part of something, which didn't fit in. And the only other thing that didn't fit in to this particular funfair was the disappearance of his brother. Put it together and there was a more than even chance that the two oddities were connected. He stopped short to avoid bumping into Peri, who had stopped short to avoid bumping into the Doctor, who had stopped short with an air of finality to look up at a looming, sinister shape before him.

Towering into the sky, in the shape of an almost life-size rocket was the latest ride at the fair – 'Space Mountain' was emblazoned across the hull, which was the front for the body of the ride behind. Giant tail-fins stretched twenty, thirty feet up, then the sleek needle shape carried on another hundred feet above that.

With a caution born of near certainty, the Doctor made his way slowly towards the entrance hatch, approached by a metal ramp up to the ticket office. As he disappeared into the hull of the spacecraft, Peri hurried after him, and Kevin after her.

The picture on the wall remained as Kevin went hesitantly inside the spaceship hull, and then faded as the Mandarin turned off the VDU. He turned to Stefan, a look of disappointment on his face. 'This is almost too easy. Time has done nothing to sharpen his wits after all.'

'You know him, Lord?' asked Stefan, unsure he understood.

'Oh yes, Stefan,' smiled the Mandarin. 'The Doctor and I are old friends.'

'I shall prepare to greet him, Lord.'

The Mandarin turned to him and smiled broadly. 'Do that, Stefan. Make everything ready. I have waited centuries for this . . .'

Chapter Three

Inside the spacecraft was a steep ramp with guardrails, turning back on itself several times to provide a series of Z ramps up into the bowels of the ride. The lighting was bright and efficient, echoing the theme of the spaceship outside, grey-painted aluminum walls, shiny metal porthole fittings and simulated computer displays flashing like a manic fruit machine paying out jackpots only.

The Doctor stopped at the top of the first ramp, before it made its turn. 'Not very popular, is it?' he remarked idly. They were the only ones in view, neither of them having noticed Kevin hovering below.

'It's hardly the high season,' pointed out Peri.

'Still, you'd expect –'

He broke off as a couple of teenagers entered at a run and raced past them, giggling, up into the ride. The Doctor shrugged.

'I never did enjoy paranoia very much, anyway.' He continued up the ramp. 'Unlike most of my contemporaries, for whom it's a *raison d'être* . . .' He stopped and cocked his head to one side.

'Can you still hear it?' asked Peri, in a whisper.

'Not now.' The Doctor shook his head and pursed his lips, then slowly trudged his way up the next ramp.

'What sort of voice is it?' asked Peri.

'Siren song, I suppose. Male or female, I can't tell. Maybe I should lash myself to the mast, just to be on the safe side.' He smiled thinly at the thought.

'Where does it come from, this voice?'

'That is rather what I'm trying to discover,' he replied, not quite gritting his teeth.

'But where . . . I mean, exactly where was the last call coming from? Direction? Distance?'

They had rounded the last corner and the platform for the ride lay before them. It was rather like a mini version of an Underground Station platform, a tube tunnel with a single platform on one side and two sets of circular doors blocking off the rest of the line at each end. The platform was now quite crowded, thirty or forty people waiting for the next ride, a shiny set of guardrails keeping them back from the platform's edge.

'Just about where we're standing, I'd say,' the Doctor replied, casually. Too casually for Peri's taste, and she looked nervously around her.

'See anything?' she asked, somewhat unnecessarily.

'I'm not looking that hard,' confessed the Doctor, although he, like Peri, was looking around all the time. By now people were pushing past them from behind, and they were both feeling distinctly in the way.

'Nothing else for it, I suppose,' shrugged the Doctor, and they both made their way to the ticket booth at the barrier to the ride.

With a smash and a clatter, the doors at one end of the tunnel burst open and the train arrived, fitting the platform exactly and pulling up to a sharp halt. More alert now than ever, the Doctor looked around, examining the disembarking passengers carefully. They were exactly what might be expected from a fairground ride, indeed they could have been the same crowd who had shared the rollercoaster with him, and some of them were. None, however, looked sinister or even familiar, so the Doctor shrugged to Peri once more, then moved off to spend the last of Jamie's hardwon cash on a couple of tickets. There was no reason in the world for them to take any notice at

34

all of Kevin, as he dug in his pocket to do the same . . .

'We're being followed,' muttered the Doctor as he and Peri moved off to join the waiting crowd, who were edging forward impatiently now as the train was being cleared of its previous passengers.

'Who by?' asked Peri, ungrammatically, but most succinctly.

'The young gentleman behind you,' replied the Doctor, softly, and then he squeezed her arm tightly in time to stop her looking round. 'Don't look round,' he told her, in case she'd missed the point. Kevin was forced to stand right next to her as the latecomers behind him pushed forward, then the Doctor's head snapped round to the tunnel entrance as he obviously heard the voice again. Involuntarily, he took a couple of strides forward, straining to identify the voice, or the direction, or both.

Peri was about to start after him when the ride attendant, seeing what he thought was a matched pair in Peri and Kevin, ushered them both into the waiting car, taking Peri's weak protest as a sign of typical feminine nerves. Women's Lib had not yet reached the inner fringes of Blackpool funfair society . . . Anyway, there was nothing much for Peri to protest at, just a mildly self-conscious move across the seat away from Kevin as the attendant pulled the safety bar across their laps.

The Doctor looked around, seemingly disorientated by the fierce concentration necessary for his audial search, and he made to join Peri – there was plenty of room on the seat with Kevin, but at that moment a harsh warning buzzer sounded and the train started to move off.

'But –' said the Doctor, helplessly, watching Peri turn desperately in her seat to look at him.

35

'Too late, mate,' said the attendant, laconically and almost prophetically and before the Doctor could frame a suitable reply, the voice came again.

'Doctor . . .'

He looked around wildly and then saw Peri looking at him just as wildly before she vanished through the double doors and into the black tunnel of the ride proper.

The ride boss, a more mature version of the laconic youth now approached the Doctor.

'Not to worry, sir,' he smiled, 'there's another car here.' And indeed, the next train had already come through the opposite doors and had pulled up at the platform. The boss even helped the Doctor down into his seat and pulled the safety bar across his lap. There was a loud click as the mechanism locked and, to the astonishment of the Doctor and, indeed, the other waiting passengers, the train moved off with the Doctor as the only passenger. He turned frantically in his seat, unable to budge the so-called safety bar and looked furiously at the ride boss, who waved him an ironic *bon voyage*. The train, and the Doctor, vanished through the doors.

The boss turned to the protesting crowd still waiting for a ride. 'Just a routine inspection, folks; management, you know?' The crowd, who had some experience of 'management' understood in a thoroughly disgruntled way and, before they could query the wild appearance of the 'management' figure they had just seen take a whole train to himself, the boss had shrugged broadly and turned back to go through one of the doors marked 'Private Staff Only' and, as though he had never been there at all, disappeared from view.

The Doctor now sat philosophically in his seat, arms folded defiantly. The train trundled slowly up a steep gradient, giving him plenty of time to observe the winking lights depicting the heavens. Which part of the heavens, he had no idea. He was very familiar with all the astronomical maps of the skies visible from Earth with the naked eye, but this bore no relation to any of them. Either it was the usual designer's botch-up or . . . or it was part of an alien sky . . .

The thought progressed no further, for the Doctor realised that in a quite unastronomical way, the sky had come to an end, or rather, the stars had. He just had time to register that all that lay ahead was in the blackest Stygian gloom when the car gave a stomach-wrenching lurch and hurtled downwards into a darkness that was as absolute as any he had ever known . . .

The Mandarin observed the picture on the VDU with an air of detachment, almost of precognition. The Space Mountain train had pulled back into its station, and Peri had disembarked onto the platform, so preoccupied with her search for the Doctor that she failed to notice Kevin hovering conspicuously near her, more and more isolated as the rest of the crowd drifted away.

'Like pieces on a board, my Lord, you plot their every move exactly.' Stefan's voice was unpleasantly gloating, whilst the Mandarin's reply was very matter-of-fact.

'Their predictability makes for a dull game, I fear.' He smiled broadly, suddenly. 'But then, they still don't know they're playing, do they?'

'What instructions shall I give for the girl, Lord?'

'We must wait, mustn't we? She will make her way to us soon enough, with that tiresome young man in attendance.'

He continued watching, idly, as Peri, after some hesitation, made her way towards the attendant and started talking to him urgently. The attendant shook his head and shrugged. Peri continued, obviously more agitated. The young man's shrugs became more pronounced, and the Mandarin smiled.

The tunnels the Doctor was walking through had the same lighting as others in the complex, but the feel of the exposed brickwork was decidedly Victorian. He'd been walking now for what he thought was about half a mile and had seen several variations on the same theme. He had concluded, correctly, that new tunnels had been added to old, bypassing others and generally developing an anthill-like feel to the whole construction. He did not award it high marks for aesthetic value, but then considered that aesthetics were low on the list of the builders' priorities. Certainly aesthetics were a long way from the minds of the gentlemen who accompanied him – one in front, one behind – if their utilitarian cover-alls and snub-nosed semi-automatic rifles were anything to go by. Comforting at least to note that the accoutrements were very twentieth-century Earth technology . . . He carried on with such idle thoughts as he took in all the other observations, and had opted for a critical standpoint, as this came easiest to him, especialy in moments of stress.

'. . . and, efficient though any service area might be, I do think you should consider improving your braking system once you've branched the line. I very nearly flew over the handlebars, you know . . .' said the Doctor aloud. The mild admonishment seemed not to hurt or wound either of the guards and the Doctor stopped to try and emphasise the gravity of his complaint.

'And that's another thing – those safety bars. Did you know they've got nasty little bumps and grooves on the top? And the ones on that wonderful rollercoaster thing too. Now they might well enhance the design features . . .'

Whether they did or not seemed not to interest the guards. They were probably weak on design theory and probably always had been, for the one behind simply prodded the Doctor with his automatic until the Doctor took the hint and started walking again. The Doctor was not so easily distracted from his self-appointed mission to inform and educate, for he continued in the same patient vein.

'Did I ever tell you about my design theory?' There was no response from the guards, but the Doctor suspected that he had indeed not let them in on it. He decided that in the interest of the pangalactic dissemination of knowledge through culture, now was as good a time as any. 'It mainly concerns the fluid lines provoked by the ergonomic imperatives . . .'

On the station platform, a now-harassed ride boss had joined the harassed attendant. Peri, when she put her mind to it, could make quite a fuss. Truth to tell, she could make quite a fuss without any mental effort at all, but now she had pulled all the stops out and the business of the ride was slowly grinding to a halt.

'People do not just disappear!' she said, loudly, as if trying to educate the ride boss to a little known fact with which he had been, until now, unfamiliar.

The boss replied with a fervour of righteous indignation befitting a Senior Fellow witnessing his latest theory being hijacked for the very first time. 'That's what I've been telling *you*, lass!' he spluttered, waving his arms in an alarming fashion. 'There is no way anyone can get off this ride between *there* –' he pointed both his arms in dramatic fashion at the doors through which the Doctor had disappeared – 'and *there*.' Now he pointed at the opposite doors, through which the Doctor should have appeared, just like the rest of the world taking the ride. 'Now is there?' he finished, challenging her to dispute her own theory.

'I think we'd better go to the Police,' said Kevin.

'And who the hell are you?' yelped the boss, which was just as well, because Peri had been about to yelp exactly the same thing, which wouldn't have helped matters at all.

'A friend, that's all,' replied Kevin with all the modesty the claim deserved. 'If you won't take this seriously,' he continued airily, 'we'll just have to find someone who will.'

'All right, all right.' The boss admitted defeat, though to what or whom he couldn't have said. 'Look, I'm up to my ears in it 'ere,' and the ever gathering crowd bore testimony to that. 'You go and talk to the Security Department. They've got the authority. Through that door there and second on the right.' Peri contrived to look both defiant and victorious and ended up looking very suspicious indeed. Kevin took her by the arm and propelled her towards the door the boss had pointed to, the one with the Staff Only sign on it. The moment the door had closed behind them, she turned on Kevin.

'Well, who *are* you, my "friend"?'

Before Kevin could frame a suitable answer, which might have taken some time anyway, the 'second on the right' the boss had mentioned swung open and another living boiler suit appeared, automatic in hand.

'A right pain in the neck, that's who,' volunteered the boiler suit. His identically dressed companion behind him grinned in agreement. 'We'd better take you somewhere and have your complaint dealt with, hadn't we?' He made an abrupt gesture with the automatic down the corridor. With a sigh of resignation, Peri, who was well used to this sort of situation, moved off without further comment. Kevin, to whom this sort of

40

thing was, to say the least, novel, was about to try an opening conversational gambit when he was actively discouraged by a harsh poke in the ribs from the second man's gun. So he also moved off behind Peri, down the sloping corridor and deeper into the complex beneath the funfair . . .

The tunnel door in the Data Room swung open and the security guard entered, closely followed by the Doctor and the other security guard. The Doctor took one look at the computers and analysers and whooped with glee.

'Oh, I say! How much is it to go on one of *these*?' He started forward towards the closest terminal and was pounced on by the two guards. Stefan took a couple of steps closer, apparently not at all pleased that the machines were being equated with the games upstairs. His opinion of the wild-eyed multi-coloured freak in front of him evidently dropped below zero, for he fixed him with his most disdainful look as he ordered the guards.

'Take him to his quarters. Our Lord is not yet ready to receive him.'

'Your Lord!' exclaimed the Doctor. 'That's either very religious or very subservient, and you don't look the religious type . . .' Which wasn't, strictly speaking, true, as the Doctor would have been forced to agree under different circumstances. Stefan looked definitely religious, in a cold-eyed, fanatic way, much the same as perhaps Rasputin might have done. Signalling both his disagreement and his impatience, Stefan snapped his fingers at the guards who proceeded to bear the Doctor away.

'Oh, I say, steady on, no offence and all that –' the Doctor wailed to no effect as he was carted off. Stefan's lip curled in a classic gesture of contempt. Clearly this clown was no match for the impeccable skill of his Lord.

*

The trudge from Space Mountain to wherever they were being taken was longer than either Peri or Kevin had expected. They had slowed gradually to a dawdle, and the guards seemed content to let them go at their own pace. Some way back they had passed a branch which was obviously close to the real world outside -- they could hear the noise of the fair and the chatter of the crowds quite clearly, and the guard in front had stood very determinedly at the junction and waited for them both to pass. He had stayed back with his friend, whether from sloppiness or design it was difficult to tell.

Kevin had taken the opportunity to bring Peri up to date on his story so far, and for so long had had no one to discuss his theories with that he quite forgot to ask her what she was doing in the middle of all this.

' . . . and this mob are obviously behind the whole thing,' he concluded, a fact which Peri thought so blindingly obvious that she forbore even to agree with him. 'If it's this well organised,' he continued, 'no wonder the police didn't find anything.'

'Looks like we're doing better than that,' replied Peri, for once in a positive frame of mind, 'but what we're going to do with whatever we *do* find . . .' The strain of positive thought proved too much; the guard immediately behind seemed to think positive was bad as well, and out of boredom as much as anything he drawled:

'Cut the cackle and get a move on!'

They both grimaced and speeded up, but only a little.

The Doctor looked down at the flap at the bottom of the door, and the little shelf below it and pondered for a moment as to what purpose it might serve. Before he could come to any useful conclusion, the guard shoved him rudely further down the corridor: three doors further down, to be exact. There was a flap but no shelf on his door, he noticed, as the other guard opened it up with an enormous and intricate key. Definitely neo-Gothic, decided the Doctor with a measure of satisfaction. He had no further time for reflection before he was pushed into the room.

'Can't you just say please?' he snarled at the guard, who simply slammed the door from the outside. The Doctor looked around his cell with a familiarity bordering on contempt. Flagstone floor, damp brick walls, truckle bed against one wall and a naked bulb hanging from the ceiling.

'Prison cells,' he snorted. 'Seen one, you've seen them all.' He turned to shout at the ever-so-firmly-shut door: 'You want to know my theory about the design of prison cells? They're all made just to keep *little* minds *out*!' The only reply to this somewhat egotistical observation was the sound of two pairs of boots receding down the corridor. The Doctor looked briefly around the cell again, noting the efficiency and reliability of the Victorian construction, and then remarked, with a note of resignation, 'And big minds quite definitely *in* . . .'

Peri noticed, with some apprehension, that the tunnel was changing. The wide, modern construction had given away to more and more brick and bare rock, with makeshift supports and sections to hold up the whole edifice. They went through a solid, old iron flood or fire door, rusted open, and beyond that was evidence of how far the modern reconstruction had reached – twentieth-century electrical conduit boxes ran the whole length of the section, and, as they rounded a corner, they came across a site which had been abandoned, by the look of it, only for the night. A section of the conduit was hanging off the wall, the spaghetti of the wires dangling from it, part attached to junction boxes, part just hanging free. A service trolley stood, half full of tools and spare parts, the top clad in sheet metal with a small vice mounted, the whole acting as a workbench as well as supply vehicle. Peri suddenly collapsed against the trolley, rolling it half a foot with her weight.

'It's no good,' she gasped, 'I can't breathe –'

Kevin dropped to her side quickly, and the security guard hurried forward.

'What's up? Get back, you –' His further instructions to Kevin ended in a sharp yelp as Peri swung the big adjustable spanner she had grabbed from the trolley full-crack against the guard's wrist. He dropped his gun with no choice in the matter at all, and was about to launch into a series of hair-curling expletives when Kevin scooped up the weapon and opened fire.

The closest Kevin had ever got to firearms prior to this had been a copy of *Rambo*, hired from the local video shop, and the film had left a lasting impression. As with so many imitators, he had carefully ignored the fact that Mr Stallone had been surrounded not so much by enemy forces as a very talented and professional bunch of special effects men. As his finger hit the trigger of the very modern and very sophisticated weapon, several things became instantly clear to him and everyone else in the tunnel.

First, automatic means pretty well that. The gun in his hand was a variation on the Ingersoll favoured by the British Special Forces once upon a time, and this model was chucking bullets down the spout at the rate of half a dozen every second.

Second, bullets chucked down the spout tended to carry on travelling until they hit something, and, depending on what that something was, they either kept on travelling or stopped. As Kevin was spraying the thing round like a garden hose, he mercifully missed everything but the tunnel walls, which even he couldn't miss, and then he started learning about ricochets. By the time he had taken his finger off the trigger, each bullet had bounced a couple of dozen times off different parts of the walls and the air was alive with very hot and very hard metal.

Third, the noise made by a large number of exploding cartridges and ricocheting bullets in the confines of a tunnel only seven or eight feet in diameter is *dreadful* and not conducive to careful or considered actions.

Which probably explained the frantic way in which Peri, the two guards and, eventually, Kevin himself, hurled themselves behind anything that offered the slightest protection from the swarm of hornets buzzing around the place. The moment the firing stopped, which was only a moment after it had started, Peri was scooting off down the corridor and round the next bend, and Kevin was scooting after her. The second boiler suit passed his partner, nursing his injured hand and moaning, and, taking careful aim, loosed off two shots after the fleeing couple. Ironically, the true professional had no more success than the rank amateur, although the two ricocheting bullets were at least this time whizzing round the targets rather than the marksman. The man on the floor reached up and dragged the gun arm down.

'No, you fool,' he spat out. 'They're not supposed to die! Not *yet*!'

The Doctor bent to his task with renewed effort. Every scrap of his extra-terrestrial power had been brought to bear on the problem in hand, and if this didn't work, then nothing would. Even the highest intellect and deftest hand could do only so much, and there were the Universal Laws of Time and Space which gave way to no being, great or small.

He looked again at the massive lock and looked again at the bent hairpin in his hand. Facing up to reality, for once, he adopted a far more constructive course of action by crossing over to the bed, lying down on it, and trying for forty winks.

Peri and Kevin crept round the next corner with a great deal more circumspection than when they had raced round the last. Here as well there was evidence of reconstruction, though in this instance of a heavier, more basic nature. The tunnel wall was being bricked up – what looked like an old spur was blocked off – and the new bricks stopped short of the roof by a foot and a half. At the foot of the new wall was a pile of bricks, bags of mortar mix and a wheelbarrow. Using this as cover, they gratefully sank down for a moment's rest, Kevin keeping a careful eye on the tunnel behind them, his acquired gun at the ready, much to Peri's concern.

'You all right?' she asked.

'Yeah, it just nicked me. I never been shot at before,' he announced with something approaching satisfaction. The lesson on ricochets had been pressed home at first hand, so to speak.

'Have you ever shot at anyone else before?' asked Peri, getting to the heart of the matter in one.

'No,' replied Kevin, making absolutely no bones about it.

'I didn't think so,' muttered Peri.

'I thought I did pretty well, first time out,' Kevin said, defensively.

'You nearly shot everyone in sight, first time out,' Peri pointed out. 'You and me included.'

'Don't knock it,' he muttered. 'It worked.'

'It did that,' agreed Peri, cheerfully. 'You want me to look at that?' She gestured at the torn sleeve of his jacket.

'No, it's all right, really,' he reassured her. 'Where are they?'

'Thinking twice about coming round that bend, I should think,' suggested Peri. 'So would I with Wild Bill Hickock waiting for me . . .' She managed a weak smile. 'More to the point, where's everyone else?' She gestured at the pile of workmen's tools and materials behind which they were sheltering. There was just enough light for Kevin to consult his wristwatch.

'Half past knocking-off time,' he offered. 'Doesn't anyone do overtime any more?'

'Maybe just as well,' replied Peri, 'We don't know whose side they'd be on anyway.'

'True enough,' agreed Kevin. 'You can bet that lot –' he gestured down the tunnel the way they'd come – 'won't be on their own next time. We'd better be getting on.'

'Down there?' asked Peri, looking down the tunnel, which ran into damp and forbidding gloom further along.

'Not much choice, is there?' Kevin pointed out. 'Come on.' Keeping a careful eye still behind them, he gently pushed her on ahead of him.

The Doctor's face appeared out of nowhere, upside down. From a mouse's point of view, it must have been one of the great heart-stopping moments of all time. However, nothing was there, not even, at this point, a friendly mouse. He hauled himself back up again and, standing now on the bed, reached up to the old cast-iron pipe which ran through the cell just below the ceiling, and tried to rattle it. The movement was only slight, and he had no plan in mind for a rattling pipe anyway, especially one that seemed as fixed and as substantial as the rest of the construction. With a sigh, he threw himself down on the bed again, fingers locked behind his head. He stared with distaste at the remote-control monitoring camera, mounted high in the corner, which was pointing directly at him. It looked back, unwaveringly, without embarrassment.

'Don't hurry on my account,' muttered the Doctor, unable now to stop his teeth clenching. In a louder and clearer voice he continued, 'You just let me know when you're ready. If I expire of boredom before that, I hope you take it very personally.' Thus miffed, he turned himself violently onto his side and seemed to go to sleep.

Kevin and Peri were hurrying down the corridor now, caution sacrificed to speed. They had both heard men's voices behind them a few moments ago, and knew their pursuers were not far behind, emboldened perhaps by the lack of the hosepipe firing from the fleeing couple. Suddenly Kevin, who was leading now, stopped. Peri lifted her head wearily and saw why. In front of them the tunnel branched into a Y.

'What do we do?' asked Peri. 'Toss a coin?'

'Nope,' replied Kevin with an unexplained note of satisfaction in his voice.

'You're not thinking of stopping and fighting it out, are you?' queried Peri with a great deal of apprehension.

'Don't be daft,' replied Kevin with a chuckle. 'I wouldn't know what to do with this thing,' he hefted the gun in his hand.

'There are quicker and easier ways of becoming a collander,' agreed Peri.

Kevin turned and knocked the gun barrel against another of the solid iron flood doors, set this time into the side of the tunnel. It gave a deep but hollow thud. 'Well,' he offered, 'we know what lies down there –' he gestured back the way they had come – 'and by now they will have organised something to come down there –' he gestured at the way they had to go if they stayed with either of the tunnels in front of them. 'So why not take a chance?'

'I can think of a hundred good reasons,' shivered Peri, wondering what on earth would be behind the great metal door. The voices behind them grew louder, and she gripped Kevin's arm tighter, nodding down the tunnels in front of them, to where the gloom was now broken by advancing torch beams.

Kevin swung the big cantilevered bolt-action mechanism on the door, which opened smoothly and easily on well oiled hinges and, after a moment's look for reassurance at each other, they went through. The door closed behind them with a surprisingly heavy, and definitely final, thud . . .

Chapter Four

Whilst the Doctor's pose might have resembled that of an Egyptian mummy, nothing else about the Doctor did. Tousled mop of hair, multi-coloured coat, old and much-loved boots, none of these belonged in the depths of a pyramid, though that's just where they might as well be, he mused. He had set himself down to the third level of *banji-rana*, one heart slowed almost to a standstill, body temperature almost three degrees down, respiration normal, and allowed the twenty per cent of brain function left to him to wander as freely as it wished. The theory was absolutely sound, and the resulting washing of impurities from his several subconscious levels should have done wonders for his powers of concentration, but it wasn't working out that way and the present state of sublimity he had achieved was driving him potty. Well, all things are relative, he was forced to concede. He had missed out a couple of stages somewhere, he knew, and the end result was nowhere near as relaxing as it should be. Probably something to do with that infernal pipe rattling, he thought irritably. Disturbing my concentration, rubbing my aura up the wrong way. The fact that *banji-rana* was designed to overcome exactly such things as rattling pipes, he found deliciously perverse, which was another sign the trance was not effective, and another very good reason why, with all the temptations it otherwise offered, he had never become a transcendentalist.

Curse that infernal pipe! With the money invested in this tunnel complex, you'd think they could have got a decent plumber . . . His eyes snapped open and the second heart tripped in full pelt. This is not the recommended method of coming out of a *banji-rana* trance, in fact for anyone with a normal human physique it was guaranteed one hundred per cent fatal, but by jove it was *fast* . . .

Not a plumber born could have cured that pipe. No water that ever fell from heaven ever produced *that* rhythmic tone. The Doctor listened for a few seconds longer.

'Ask not for whom the pipe clangs,' he muttered, with only a pitiful gesture of an apology to Mr Donne, as he frantically searched through his pockets for something to communicate with. He uttered a small cry of triumph as he pulled forth an ancient pair of nutcrackers.

'The right tool for the right job,' he crowed as he jumped up on the bed. Hesitantly, he tapped out a short staccato beat of his own devising on the pipe. Silence. He tried another variation, slightly less mathematical. Silence. He thought for a moment and tried a bongo beat he'd picked up with Livingstone. Nothing. At last, reduced to childish basics he tried a straightforward, no-mucking-about, this-one's-for-you-baby, one-two-three. Not a peep.

'Not the Abbe Faria then,' he concluded, glumly. Determined to put on at least as good a show as the Count of Monte Cristo, he started tapping again.

Kevin was in the process of discovering several salient facts about the design parameters of throw-away gas lighters. They gave off a very poor level of ambient illumination; they promised not to last for long if kept on continuously; and after a remarkably short time, however carefully they were handled, they started to singe whichever finger was holding the gas trigger

51

down. With a muttered curse, he was forced to release the button and blow on his slightly toasted fingers.

'Maybe this wasn't such a good idea,' ventured Peri, as they waited patiently for the umpteenth time for Kevin's fingers to resume normal body heat.

At last Kevin summed up in a few short words his feelings of the past twenty minutes: 'Better than being shot.'

'Marginally,' replied Peri, rubbing one of half a dozen bumps she'd picked up since they'd started down this tunnel. Unlike the others, faced as they had been in brick or metal, this tunnel was carved out of the bare rock, with a very uneven floor and walls that seemed to have been constructed with an obstacle course in mind. Worst of all, this one had no light at all, and what would happen if they ran out of gas before they ran out of tunnel, Peri shuddered to think. Lost in the dark, hundreds of feet underground. It had to be one of her least favourite nightmares. 'How are your fingers?' she asked, more out of fear of the dark than any genuine concern for her companion's well-being.

'Medium-rare,' he replied, glumly. 'Give us another minute.'

Which Peri would have quite willingly done had not at that moment a slow, grinding, whirring sound a foot from her right elbow made her jump a yard and a half to her right. Which sent her crashing into Kevin, taking him somewhat by surprise, and flinging the lighter, unbidden, from his already suffering fingers.

'What's that?' she cried.

'The lighter!' he swore, at just the same moment.

His fear became hers as they both scrambled around with their hands on the rough floor of the tunnel.

The grinding was joined by another, not far behind from the sound of it, and Peri spun her head to try and make out something of the threat. Another whirring and another, a smashing sound, a hit, a rasping sound. They were surrounded. She caught her breath, not knowing which way to turn next. The grind became a whirr and the rasp became a crackle and as though a shaft of light had broken through the darkness, the strains of 'My Darling Clementine' came on at full belt. So did the lights, as something, or someone, threw a master switch.

Peri and Kevin looked around them in absolute amazement. They were in what appeared to be the main gallery of an old mine, dozens of feet high, scores of feet long and, below them, a drop to the floor that had 'broken neck' written all over it. Literally. 'Broken Neck Gap' was written roughly on a board. Off in the middle distance they could see a brazier, glowing and smoking in front of a workman's hut, and, on the other side of the gallery, a metal truck, open-topped, was trundling past on its rails. From where they stood they could see twenty or so miners, half life-size, working the mother lode.

'It's the gold mine ride,' exclaimed Kevin. 'We're right in the middle of the new gold mine ride!'

They both burst out laughing, more out of relief than anything particularly humorous. The old Forty-Niner a couple of feet away from Peri, whose stirring into life had caused her such panic, had a distinct twinkle painted into his eye, but for all that he looked as tough as old boots, and not given to much casual humour: he raised and lowered the pickaxe he was wielding with a grim determination that was gold fever through and through.

'Which way now?' gasped Peri as the laughter died away.

'Ask him,' suggested Kevin with a grin, gesturing at the old-timer. Peri bent to speak in the figure's ear.

'Er – 'scuse me, sir. Which way to the nearest Police Station?' She bent to hear his answer, then straightened up, a triumphant grin on her face.

'Well?' asked Kevin.

'Follow the Yellow Brick Road, of course,' replied Peri cheerfully.

'Come on then,' said Kevin, 'it can't be far now, and at least we can see where we're going without cooking ourselves.' They set off down what they had thought was a tunnel, but which had for a hundred yards or more been the bed on which the ride cars would come when the place was open, judging from the rails.

As they went, the old miner stopped his work with the pick-axe and turned his head to follow them . . .

The Doctor's eyes blinked in rapid unison with the return tapping on the pipe.

'At last,' he breathed. The tapping stopped and he started his own, a logarithmic variation of 'Three Blind Mice' with base two as its starting point. Anyone should be able to get that, he surmised, and once they'd established a rapport, they could exchange information, compare notes, and devise some way of getting out of this wretched place, but first they had to start *communicating*. The pipe was overwhelmed by a rapid peppering of taps. The Doctor stopped and listened. He could detect no pattern-recognition code at all.

'Just my luck,' he complained bitterly, 'banged up with a fellow prisoner who doesn't even know "Three Blind Mice" . . .'

Kevin was showing signs of strain. He was starting to talk. After all this time, it was something to have someone to talk *to*, particularly after the events of the past few hours, and he had filled Peri in on most of his conversation with the Police, most of his life before that, and the complete story of his family and their funny ways. He was just going back over the highlights of the past couple of weeks.

'. . . and everything seemed to be happening near that video arcade place. The lights, the Mandarin, that red thing whatever it was, and me brother Geoff. The time I spotted him, and I swear it was him, he was with this fellah dressed all in black. Just my idea of a Mafia hit man, he was. Tall and threatenin' and – you know, dressed all in black . . .'

Peri had long ago learned from the Doctor not to go entirely on how a person dressed – an essential freedom of the intellect whenever undertaking intergalactic or transdimensional travel – but she wasn't about to tell Kevin that. She was, in any case, too busy looking around her to take much notice of what the boy was rattling on about. She was convinced they were being followed. Or watched. Or led into a trap. Something. Anything. It just felt *wrong*.

'It all leads back to that arcade,' pronounced Kevin, sagely.

'Well this doesn't lead back to that arcade,' pointed out Peri, somewhat sniffily. 'And the Doctor didn't vanish in the arcade and we didn't get shot at in the arcade . . .' In the cause of rebuttal, this seemed overkill, even to her. She changed tack. 'Say, how come they switched this thing on –' she made a gesture to take in the whole elaborate edifice of the model gold mine – 'just when we walked into it?'

'Oh come on,' protested Kevin, 'I thought I was supposed to be the paranoid.'

'I always get paranoid when people are hunting me,' admitted Peri, glumly.

'They didn't switch it on just when we came in – it just got switched on, that's all.'

55

'Well come on then,' snapped Peri, 'I just want to get out of here and into some nice friendly Police Station before someone decides to switch it all off again . . .' And with that she strode off down the track.

Kevin, with a sigh, followed her.

The three miners far below them, in a tableau round a camp fire, turned and craned their necks to watch them go . . .

The Doctor was still trying to conduct the ferrous conversation with his distant friend, but since conversation is by definition a two-way process, he was not meeting with much success. In fact, he still hadn't got to first base, and, as far as he could tell, neither had his friend. In desperation, and sacrificing every jot of his intellectual pride, which was very considerable, he had even gone over to bashing out standard Morse Code. No effect whatsoever. His friend obviously wasn't a military type either, nor a radio ham, but that still left an awful lot of possibilities . . .

The tapping from the other end suddenly took on an urgent, then a frantic rhythm.

'Full of sound and fury, signifying nothing,' said the Doctor bitterly, remembering a rather neat turn of phrase he'd once given away in a London pub for nothing more than a jug of ale.

The tapping, suddenly and decisively, stopped.

'Well, my friend, I wonder what interrupted *your* transmission?' speculated the Doctor, softly. There was no reply.

The Great Gallery of the mine had narrowed to a tiny passage, through which the ride train would trundle, they supposed, giving a sense of claustrophobia where the Gallery had done the opposite. Niches let into the rock displayed other scenes of mining life – a couple of bunk beds in one, a table and four miners carousing in another, and the lighting to match had become much more directional and atmospheric. Peri tried to take that into account when she shivered, and failed miserably. There was still something very wrong . . .

She stopped, suddenly, tugging Kevin's arm as she did so.

'What's up?'

'Sssh!'

They froze for a moment.

'What is it?' he insisted.

'I heard someone following us.' She stood very still, listening intently. Kevin studied her carefully for a moment. He turned his head to look back the way they had come. The sounds from the Gallery and the rest of the goldmine were more distant now. There were three distinct crunches, like heavy boots on gravel, and then . . . nothing.

'Come on, you're beginning to spook me now,' Kevin complained nervously. 'It's just the ride – the workings – whatever –' The attempt to shrug it off did not work, largely because of the way he hefted the gun in his hand and pulled off the safety catch. He took her hand, and led off, at a rather faster pace now.

They left behind a grizzled old miner, pan in hand, swishing gravel in and out of a thin stream of water. A moment after they had gone, he put the pan down and reached for a geologist's hammer by his side, a flat end to one side of the head and a wicked looking curved spike on the other. He swung the hammer expertly and then, moving very carefully, the three-foot high figure moved off after them.

The Doctor sighed and leaned his shoulder disconsolately against the wall. He raised his nutcrackers and gave a despondent couple of bangs on the pipe. There

57

was still no reply. He turned sharply as he heard the approach of several measured footsteps in the corridor outside. The pipe started to clang again, the same frantic cacophony that had been interrupted before. The footsteps became more measured, more military as they drew nearer, then came to a sudden and precise stop right outside his cell door.

All pretence of cool had been cast aside now as Peri and Kevin hurried through the dim tunnels. The noise of the rest of the mine was far off now, just the strains of 'Darling Clementine' echoing tauntingly around them. There had been no side shows for some distance, just the rough rock of the walls and roof, lit occasionally by the flickering light of an artificial oil lamp. Ahead of them, the tracks stretched away through the narrow tunnel, a gloomy bend hiding the next section from them. They looked around as a creaking sound echoed over their heads, then a rumbling began which grew, louder and louder. Distinctly alarmed, they tried to see where the sound was coming from, but as it grew, it seemed to come from every direction at once, creaking, shifting, groaning until, with a gigantic crash, a huge section of the roof in front of them caved in.

Peri gave a shriek and ducked away from it instinctively. Kevin nobly tried to shield her from the worst of it as they waited for the crushing force of the roof-fall to bury them.

The rumbling died away. They looked up. The roof timbers had come to a stop a foot or so above their heads, criss-crossing the top half of the tunnel, held back as if by magic. By more magic, as they watched, the timbers gently and smoothly creaked back to their original position. Peri nearly laughed out loud. It was a fake fall, meant as an added thrill to the punters as they passed through on the train. With one breath she

58

sighed relief, and with another cursed the ingenuity of the ride's designers in achieving so realistic an effect. They hurried on, looking up at the trick timbers still with some apprehension as they passed underneath. They rounded the bend in the tunnel.

Past the fake fall the stunted shadows passed, one, two, three, four and then two more behind, treading softly, walking just on the railway sleepers between the lines, none of them talking, nor even whispering. Grim and purposeful they marched on, none of the figures over three feet tall . . .

Instinctively, the Doctor stepped back, then back again, until he was pressing against the cell wall and could retreat no further. The door was disappearing. From the top down, it was simply being erased in a process that by the looks of it wasn't going to take above half a minute to complete. The corridor behind seemed substantial enough, as did the first of the half-dozen tall figures standing there, then the process seemed to speed up exponentially until, with a rush, the opening was clear.

'You!' exclaimed the Doctor as the full figure of the tall man was revealed. He started to go through the door but was immediately stopped by a hard, painful, invisible barrier. He recoiled from it to see the Mandarin smile gently.

'My dear Doctor . . . Forgive these tedious formalities, but I feared your impetuous nature might bring us both to regrettable harm without some form of restraint . . .'

'*Brevity* is the soul of wit,' the Doctor pointed out, ruefully rubbing the ends of his fingers. He'd had his arms in front of him as he'd walked forward, otherwise he'd be rubbing his nose, he supposed.

'I agree entirely,' conceded the Mandarin, 'but this is no time for wit, surely? And, after all,' he continued in a reasonable and persuasive tone of voice, 'I've waited so long for this meeting that I've had plenty of time to make up five words where one would do.'

'So this is another of your absurd games?'

'Not absurd, no. I still have plenty of those, more than I know what to do with, in fact,' and he almost chuckled. 'No, this one is in deadly earnest . . .'

'Where's Peri?' demanded the Doctor, sharply.

'I should have liked to invite your charming companion to join us in the same diverting fashion as yourself, but I was rather relying on her to collect a young gentleman on her way in, which, I'm delighted to say, she has done. In her own whimsical fashion.'

'If you've harmed her –' the Doctor growled, taking a step forward, but stopping short of the invisible barrier.

'Then what, Doctor?' taunted the Mandarin.

'Then you and I shall fall out.' The Doctor spoke calmly and quietly, but the seemingly harmless words were filled with a threat that carried across the room and were not held by the invisible barrier. Stefan instinctively moved closer to his 'Lord', who stayed him with a tiny gesture of his hand.

'I assure you, my dear Doctor, she is in perfect health, merely being . . . entertained . . . by one of my minor *divertissements*, as is the young man. Over the past few weeks I have tried several interesting . . . inducements . . . to persuade him to accept my hospitality. Caution, sadly, has proven the better part of valour in his case, until, that is, Miss Peri came along. They make a very good team.'

'Oh, stop this nonsense,' interrupted the Doctor, irritated by the glacial calm, and glacial flow, of the Mandarin's words. 'They're not interested in playing any of your games, and neither am I –'

'But you haven't even started yet, Doctor,' interrupted the Mandarin in turn, 'not in earnest. And how could you, with no one to play with. Meet your opponent, Doctor.' And, as he spoke this last with some relish, the Mandarin made a slight motion with his hand, gesturing towards the wall behind the Doctor. In the same way as the door had, the wall started to dissolve, rapidly clearing from the top downwards until it had vanished, revealing a cell exactly like the Doctor's

But the occupant of the cell was not like the Doctor at all. Half spider, half crab, it stood. Its antennae were waving towards the Time Lord and its black, bulbous body was spattered with sparse coarse hairs a foot long. It was supported on five thin, hairy, angular legs and the sixth fearsome leg was no more than a single armoured claw, whose inside edges were serrated and stained with the blood of countless gory meals . . .

The tight-fitting tunnel had once again broadened to a gallery, though not as grand as the one they'd first seen. Kevin was breathing heavily now, and Peri, being pulled along by his hand more than helped by it, was panting as well.

'Doesn't this damned ride ever end?' she protested, as the gallery revealed itself.

'You certainly get your money's worth,' observed Kevin, ruefully.

She forced him to a stop as they both recovered a little of their breath. 'Isn't there a service hatch, or something?' she gasped.

'How d'you think we got in here?' he replied, with a note of bitterness.

'Then maybe that's the way to get out.'

'What d'you think I've been looking for for the past half mile?' Kevin asked in what was almost a snarl.

'Well we can't just –'

Her protest was cut off short as a lump of rock splattered against the wall near her head. As she spun to see where it had come from, another, and then another came whizzing through the air. Instinctively, she raised her arm to protect her head.

Below them was a group of six miners, who had been struggling to right an overturned trolley. They had ceased their otherwise perpetual labours now and were slowly moving up the bank towards them. Across the gallery, another pair, climbing a rock face, had settled on a ledge and were searching for more rocks. In the gloom she could see half a dozen diminutive figures moving out of the tunnel, down the track towards them, crouching low, every hand holding a rock or a weapon.

'The miners!' she gasped, incredulously. 'They've come alive!'

She and Kevin also stooped into a low crouch and half-ran, half-stumbled further along the tracks. A hail of rocks shattered all around them and, with a cry of pain, Kevin stumbled and fell, lying still on the ground with blood oozing from a wound behind his ear. Peri crouched down by him, trying to shield his body with hers, arms wrapped tightly around her head. The hail of rocks intensified and, from every side, the dwarf miners moved in for the kill.

The top half of the body was shiny carapace, sectioning and sliding together as the monster swayed in time to its waving antennae. In the softer, leprous looking lower half, which could have been all belly, a small mouth, ringed with needle teeth opened and closed, questing for food as the mandibles on either side, miniature replicas of the giant claw, seemed to wave in anticipation.

The Doctor backed further away, until with a small cry, he jerked his hand back once more from the stinging, burning, invisible wall. He could go no further. A thin chuckle came from the Mandarin, and what sounded like a jeer came from Stefan. The creature seemed to sense weakness, for the multi-faceted eyes on their stubby stalks turned towards the Doctor and the whole revolting body, two metres across, swung around to face him.

'Winner take all, Doctor,' taunted the Mandarin, the chuckle turning into a dry laugh, then he moved his hand in a curious gesture and the cell door rematerialised, becoming solid again. The Doctor raced to the door and slammed into its all too solid mass. In what he knew to be a futile appeal, he banged frantically on it with his clenched fist, to be rewarded only with a savage laugh from Stefan. He spun back to face his opponent.

Giant claw raised in preparation, the monstrosity moved forward . . .

Chapter Five

The Doctor's natural curiosity did what no amount of transcendental meditation could do – it killed his fear stone dead and gave him pause for thought. He watched the slavering beast approach and cocked his head slightly to one side. What was it? What was so odd about it?

Well, yes – discount the half crab half spider and the fact that it was six feet across. Hardly usual fauna for Blackpool-by-the-Sea, agreed. Never mind the giant claw or the horrid hairy legs, forget the eyes on stalks and the mouth. What was so *odd*?

Ah! No . . . maybe . . . Yes, that's it! That's what it is! The claw! That snapping noise it's making. The tempo it's waving about. Not exactly Klemperer, it's true, but it's the same jolly old rhythm!

With a single bound the Doctor was up on his bed again, nutcrackers in hand, as he beat out the rhythm on the pipe. The claw stopped waving immediately, the beast not bothering to turn its head. The Doctor beat out another few notes. The beast wavered again. More thumping, then with a curious sideways shuffle the monster lurched over to the pipe in the newly revealed cell and started tapping out the familiar noise of the earlier efforts at communication.

The Doctor slumped against the wall. 'See . . . ?' He called out to no one in particular, but he was certain the Mandarin was monitoring every movement in the cell. 'You can talk your way out of anything . . .'

*

Peri shook the unconscious Kevin, desperately trying to revive him. She looked up suddenly, not able to work out what had changed. Then she realised. The hail of rocks had stopped. That in itself struck Peri as suspicious, and she wondered what new tricks the murderous mannikins were up to now. Raising her head cautiously, she immediately understood. Walking carefully towards her, guns at the ready, were the two boiler suits. She shook Kevin again.

'Kevin! Kevin!' Still no response. 'I'm sorry,' she whispered, softly, then she slipped away from him and, at a crouch moved deeper in the mine, unhindered now by the miners, who seemed once again frozen into immobility.

She stayed behind an outcrop of rock and watched the boiler suits reach Kevin. One of them bent down to give the boy a cursory examination, then he took a radio from his overall pocket and started to speak into it, but whatever he said, she couldn't make out.

She turned to go, wanting to get away before whatever aid boiler suit was summoning turned up, and nearly died of fright as she stared into the weather-beaten face of another Forty-Niner. He stayed the way he should have, grinning from ear to ear, immobile. Peri took in the wicked-looking pinch-bar he was holding, and eased it from the wood and plastic fingers. She hefted it in her hand. That felt better. She set off again.

Amid the rich settings of his room, the Mandarin looked positively regal. The Doctor took time to look around the room as Stefan ushered him in, and was suitably impressed by the quality and taste of the furnishings. Stefan lead him unprotesting to stand in front of the Mandarin's giant desk, hands thrust deep into pockets, utterly disrespectful as usual. Stefan glared, furious at

65

this affront to his Lord's dignity. His Lord didn't seem to mind at all, merely raised an eyebrow a millimetre in Stefan's direction.

'The youth is being taken to the cells now, Lord,' reported the henchman in answer to the silent interrogation.

'Very well,' acknowledged the Mandarin.

'But the girl –' Stefan continued, hesitantly, reluctant to report less than total success.

'*I* am dealing with the girl,' cut in the Mandarin with a sharp edge to his voice. Stefan looked disappointed, very disappointed, and the Doctor was worried as he watched him out of the corner of his eye, only half-pretending to study the magnificent Chung silk tapestry on the wall.

'Yes, Lord.'

'Toymaker –' started the Doctor, a detectable threat in his voice.

'Oh, don't worry, Doctor,' cut in the Mandarin again, a trifle testily, thought the Doctor. Perhaps things weren't going quite as much to plan as they'd like me to think . . . Or perhaps he's fed up with leashing Stefan, the prowling hit man. Goodness knows, I would be – 'She's quite safe . . . for the moment . . .' continued the Mandarin, as if that dismissed the matter from further consideration for the next century or so.

The Doctor plonked himself without ceremony in the big chair at the side of the desk – the only other comfortable chair in the room – and insolently swung his leg over the arm, where it dangled nonchalantly. Stefan stiffened visibly, and looked as if his normal retribution for such impertinence was the amputation of the offending limb without the benefit of medical training . . .

'I don't believe you consider "safe" to be an absolute term,' offered the Doctor, idly, as if the matter might offer possibilities in philosophical discussion, but might as easily prove to be an intellectual dead-end.

'Everything is relative, is it not?' countered the Mandarin, either aping the Doctor's own oft-expressed caveat or endorsing Mr Einstein's observations with his own seal of approval.

'Depends on your standpoint,' observed the Doctor, then added, as if to demonstrate his own, more accurate interpretation of the mathematician's masterpiece, 'or rather on where you're standing . . .'

The pedantry, predictably enough, was lost on Stefan. Stefan wouldn't have known, or cared about, the General Theory of Relativity if it had come up and hit him on the back of the head with the velocity of C^2, though he would certainly have been interested in duplicating the effect on someone else's head. Preferably the tousled one lolling in the chair in front of him.

'Lord, allow me to instruct this insolent gypsy in the proper courtesies –' snarled the guard dog, ears pricking up and teeth baring. The Doctor, stung by what he took to be a derogatory attitude to his friends the travelling people, lashed out a little himself.

'Does your Myrmidon have to be here?' he snapped at the Mandarin. 'I mean, can't you get him back to his kennel?'

'I had hoped that listening to a Time Lord's wisdom might advance dear Stefan's education,' announced the Mandarin with not a scrap of sincerity in his voice.

'You've left it a little late for that,' pointed out the Doctor, and then finished, with a sniff: 'And even I need a spark of basic intelligence to work with . . .'

The Mandarin chuckled. 'Well,' he affirmed, 'Stefan's intelligence is very basic indeed.'

'And, given there's not a moral scruple in his whole body, you've got the prime requisites for the Universal

Henchman,' snapped the Doctor, irritated for an irrational moment by the ease with which his antagonists were always able to surround themselves with the dregs of whichever society they were in at the time.

'Not at all, Doctor,' disputed the Mandarin mildly. 'If those were the only requirements, I could have half the human race in my employ.' He smiled, gently, patronisingly. His eyes drifted back to Stefan and almost softened for a moment. 'No, loyalty and complete obedience are needed too, and they are far rarer qualities . . .' Stefan almost beamed with gratification. Almost. In fact his face didn't move a muscle. Just the eyes shone with a fervent, Storm-Trooper zeal.

'Nonsense,' shot back the Doctor, unwilling to let Stefan preen himself in this gruesome fashion. 'You can find them in abundance in any penal colony on any planet in any universe. They're all sadly full of madmen and their lackeys . . .'

The Mandarin rose gracefully, and placed his hands in the wide sleeves of his robes. He walked around the desk to observe more closely the tapestry which had seemed to interest the Doctor on his way in.

'Your manners, Doctor, do not have appeared to have improved with time,' he observed mildly as he crossed the room. 'I invite you and your travelling companion here to join with me in a few innocent games –'

'Since when has there ever been anything innocent about your games?' interjected the Doctor, bitterly. The Mandarin chose to ignore the remark.

'– and you do nothing but rail against the qualities of my poor servants, hardly the behaviour of a true gentleman, let alone a sportsman.'

'None of your . . . pastimes qualify as sports,' retorted the Doctor, 'and the activities in the Roman

Coliseum were also called games, as I recall . . .'

'There are similarities,' agreed the Mandarin, with a smile almost to himself.

'There certainly are. Cruel and pointless, both of them. I don't like your version any better than I liked theirs, in fact –' the Doctor stood abruptly and Stefan stiffened. – 'I don't like *you*, Toymaker, and I don't like the vacuous way you wander through this Universe treating every intelligent species you meet like counters on a board . . .' The Mandarin's comment about the Roman Games suddenly touched a nerve. 'How long have you been here?' asked the Doctor, suspiciously.

'Here?' asked the Mandarin, taking his hands from his sleeves and gesturing broadly at the whole room.

'No, here,' repeated the Doctor, raising his arm high above his head and rotating his hand to indicate the whole planet.

'Oh, not long,' replied the Mandarin, airily, 'a matter of millenia only.'

'Subjective?' asked the Doctor, darkly.

'What other kind of time is there?' asked the Mandarin innocently.

The Doctor chose not to rise to the bait. 'Enjoying it?' he asked the Mandarin, echoing the same innocent tone.

'Fascinating little world, isn't it?' continued the Mandarin, in a polite, drawing-room sort of way.

'Yes, it is.'

'A favourite of yours, I believe?'

'Yes. Is that why you came here?'

'The ingenuity of the locals is really quite remarkable . . .'

'Is that why you came here?' repeated the Doctor, a terrible suspicion forming in his mind.

'And they do so love playing games. All *sorts* of games . . .

'Have you come here for *me*?' The question was now insistent.

'My dear Doctor!' The Mandarin swung round, the polite tone of voice now belied by the glint in his eye. 'The last time we met you were the victim of your own intellectual conceit, which now seems to have developed into full-blown paranoia! At one time, it's true, I held a passing interest in your . . . peregrinations . . . through time and space, but the idea that I should squat on this amusing but depressingly backward planet waiting for you to 'drop in' is egocentric in the extreme . . .'

The Doctor refused to be bluffed. 'You set up the Space-Time Vortex,' he accused, quietly.

'Doctor,' replied the Mandarin, fixing him with his eyes and replying just as quietly, 'I *am* the Space-Time Vortex.'

That stopped the Doctor in his tracks. Either the man was truly mad or . . . 'What do you want with me?' he asked, his voice a little hoarse with what could have been genuine fear.

'You know perfectly well,' replied the Mandarin implacably.

'How often do I have to win before you give up?' he demanded with a sigh.

'Oh lots,' replied the Mandarin, sweeping back to his enormous chair, having decided that whatever interested the Doctor in the tapestry was of no significance at all to himself.

'No more games,' asserted the Doctor. 'I refuse.'

'Oh just one more, Doctor. We'll call that the decider, shall we?'

'A "decider" implies the scores are even. They're not. I'm ahead. Let's just call it "the last", shall we?'

'Then you will play? Good . . .'

'Not yet,' warned the Doctor. 'Not at all unless –'

'Unless?' prompted the Mandarin.

'Unless I see Peri, safe and sound, in the flesh. Where is she?'

'Close to hand, I assure you, and having quite the time of her life . . .'

'I warned you, Toymaker . . .'

'I will not harm her,' the Mandarin protested, seeking to reassure the Time Lord and failing utterly.

'Not you or any of your . . . servants?' insisted the Doctor, shooting a look at the attendant Stefan.

'Oh, absolutely,' replied the Mandarin, opening his arms in guileless innocence, which sent a shiver of apprehension right down to the Doctor's trans-dimensional toes.

Peri held her breath and moved forward as stealthily as she knew how. A miner stood in front of her, a rifle cradled in his hands, his back turned towards her. There was no one else around in this smaller gallery by the side of the track, the scene depicting some sort of stores depot. The route out of the ride, along the tracks and away from the boiler suits and miners following her, was past the miner. And that was that. Loathing the idea of what she had to do, she nevertheless edged forward, then froze as she thought she heard something further down the track, behind her and not far away. Whatever it was moved off at a tangent, and the sound was soon lost beneath the distant but ever-present strains of 'Darling Clementine'. If ever she heard that song again, she would be rather more than 'dreadful sorry' herself . . .

The miner's back was only a foot in front of her now. Heart thumping wildly, she raised the pinch-bar she held in her hands high over her head, then took a mighty swing at the hatted head before her. To her horror, the head bounded off the shoulders and leapt a dozen feet, coming to a rest by the side of a box of ammunition, and turned towards her, still grinning evilly. She clasped a hand over her mouth. In slow motion, the body keeled over, and her eyes, with a will of their own, followed it down. Then they widened in astonishment, and she knelt to examine the torso more closely. A tangle of wires, now torn off, spread from the middle of the broken neck, their other ends protruding from the head a dozen feet away. An android. A plain, simple, common-or-garden robot! Not some frightful will-o'-the-wisp or hobgoblin come unnaturally to life, but a mere artifact. She looked down on it in contempt. But they had been so lifelike, so evidently little people, living people . . . The latter half of the twentieth century, she knew, could never produce anything so refined, so fluid so . . . *lifelike*. She heard that noise behind her again, closer now. There was nothing to be seen, but she quietly slipped behind the stacked pile of boxes and waited as still as she could. If they caught up with her, she'd give as good as they could dish out, but if it was just another of these horrid mechanical gnomes, she'd soon show it what she was made of, now that she'd found out what *they* were made of.

The sound came again, and then again. Stealthy footsteps . . . and only one of them, it sounded like. She tensed herself, hefting the trusty crowbar in antici-pation as the footsteps drew nearer, and risked a peek round the corner of the boxes. A figure was walking slowly towards her with what looked like a gun in his hands. A full-grown figure, not a dwarf. She breathed a little faster. Oh well, in for a penny, in for a pound . . . She sprang out of her hiding place, the crowbar already swinging as she moved, but the figure sidestepped easily and brought the gun up swiftly to bear on her.

'Peri!'

Kevin lowered the gun, and Peri almost passed out with relief. 'Oh, Kevin!'

'Are you all right?'

'I was about to ask you the same thing,' she replied, not altogether truthfully. Her mind was buzzing with too many other questions. 'How did you get away?' being the first of them.

'Easy,' he grinned. 'I just played dead until they went away. They called up some collection team on the radio, and left me for them. I scarpered before they arrived. If they're all that thick, then we've no problems . . .'

'They haven't seemed that thick so far,' Peri pointed out, ruefully. 'Anyone who can build androids like that – ' she gestured at the broken miner '– isn't thick at all. Did you know they were all androids?' she asked, suddenly.

'What else would they be?' grinned Kevin. 'I didn't think they'd imported a whole tribe of pygmies, just to dress up this place . . . Why?'

Peri shrugged. 'Oh, just not something you come across every day in off-season Blackpool.'

'I think I've found a way out,' grinned Kevin, crowing a little.

'At last!' sighed Peri. Kevin turned to go, but seemed to wobble a bit. 'Are you really all right?' Peri asked, concerned for a moment.

'One of them rocks caught me a proper clout, that's all. Go on, you lead the way – it's up there by the log cabin . . .' She looked up at the log cabin on the other side of the gallery, thirty or forty feet away, and started to walk towards it. With one backward glance over his shoulder, Kevin followed . . .

The Doctor noted with detached interest that the guard had to open his cell door with a very large key as he ushered him into his guest-quarters. No magic wave of the hand for him, then. The tricks department was one the Mandarin obviously kept very much to himself. Might be useful, that . . . Stefan pushed the Doctor rudely in the back, forcing him into the cell.

His eyes immediately fell on the shiny machine in the corner, all bells and whistles, or, more accurately, all screen and logos and flashing lights. It looked like big brother to one of the machines upstairs in the video arcade, and the Doctor loathed it on sight.

'What,' he demanded imperiously, 'is *that* monstrosity?'

'It is that upon which you will play your last game with my master,' replied Stefan, softly.

'Is that all?' replied the Doctor, as scathingly as he could.

'It will suffice.'

'Will it indeed?'

The Doctor looked at the machine a little more closely, but could see nothing remarkable about it. Just another mindless shoot-em-down video game . . . Stefan grinned wolfishly at the Doctor's apparent perplexity, and turned on his heel to go. 'Does room service extend to dinner?' called the Doctor to the retreating broad back. There was no break in stride, and certainly no reply as Stefan and the guard left, locking the cell door behind them with a great deal of fuss and noise, or so the Doctor thought. He shrugged and was about to turn back to examine the machine when he saw, now that Stefan was out of the way, a recumbent form on the bed. He hurried over and turned the figure over. There was a stirring and a groan as Kevin struggled to raise himself up off the bed.

The Mandarin delicately moved his fingers again on the surface of the crystal ball, activating the viewing screen again. The Doctor's attempts to bring Kevin back to consciousness were as primitive and as futile as were to be expected, which, the Mandarin thought, was good enough in the circumstances. He checked himself quickly. For a very long time, he had been promising himself never to underestimate the Doctor again. He was not about to spend another tedious length of his time-continuum waiting for his next chance.

The fingers moved again, and the scene in the goldmine swam up on the screen: Peri being followed by Kevin as they made their way cautiously past a group of miners, endlessly filling a gold-ore truck. The Mandarin smiled contentedly as he flicked between the pictures, the Doctor and Kevin, and Peri and Kevin. He did so like a good trick. And this one had a certain . . . roundness to it, a certain . . . elegance of self-fulfilment. Time to step up the game, he thought, and moved his fingers again . . .

Peri stopped near the log cabin.

'Where now?' she asked, with a sigh.

'To the left,' replied Kevin, indicating a narrow path past a couple of barrels. Peri stopped and cocked her head again. She listened for a moment or two.

'It's gone very quiet in here,' she observed, and indeed the background noise of the ride had gone down to just a few creaks and groans as the equipment settled down. Even the interminable 'Darling Clementine' was conspicuous by its absence.

'They've all knocked off,' shrugged Kevin.

'Just like that? The miners haven't knocked off, surely?'

'Waiting for the night shift to come on, eh?' answered Kevin cheerfully.

'I don't like it. Not one little bit,' protested Peri.

'Come on then,' answered Kevin, shortly, 'let's get out of here.' He motioned for her to lead the way again, and she took a breath and started walking along the path.

It wound up, along the wall of the gallery, climbing quite steeply to disappear into a fissure in the rock wall, the scene with the gold truck and cabin forming a valley between where they were now and the ride-track they'd been following since they came into the ride. Peri wondered idly just how Kevin had found this track from where she'd left him – come the back way, obviously . . .

Kevin let her walk on a little, then looked around, carefully. In the far distance, right at the end of this gallery, a boiler suit moved into sight briefly from the tunnel, just long enough to wave in Kevin's direction. After a glance at Peri's retreating back, Kevin waved back, then he turned to follow her.

For a split second he seemed to stagger off-balance and, as he did so, his head started to shimmer and fade out. The effect would have been perfectly familiar to the Doctor, who had seen the same thing happen to his cell door not too long ago, but even the Doctor would have doubted the evidence of his eyes, for in less time than it takes to blink, the shimmering had vanished and Kevin was himself again, the only detectable difference now being a wolfish grin on his face as he regarded the distant figure of the girl ahead of him, a grin that belonged far more comfortably on the face of Stefan.

Chapter Six

As with so many of these do-it-yourself jobs, reflected the Doctor, bitterly, it's the fiddly bits that take the time. It had been hard enough teasing the thread inch by inch from the old-fashioned buttons on the mattress while Kevin shielded him with his body, but now here he was, scrunched up on tip-toe in the corner of the room, still listening to the boy's life history, or what must be a good part of it, while with infinite care he tied his trusty sonic screwdriver to the side of the monitoring video camera.

'. . . and then the ruddy miners, or whatever they are, started hurling ruddy great rocks at us and here I am . . . look, what *are* you doing?'

The Doctor made the frantic signals so beloved of interviewers the world over as his right hand whirred around in Catherine Wheel fashion indicating, Keep it going . . .

'Wha'? Oh . . . yeah, all right . . . Well, before that, then, I was, er, born in Bootle, like, just outside the 'Pool, and I think me first memory must've been of me old mum bashin' the clothes wi' rocks down by the stream, 'cos we couldn't afford a spin-dryer, like . . .'

As Kevin joined most of his fellow Liverpudlians in fantasising about his humble origins and the hard but honest life of the good old days – a direct legacy of the Beatles' publicity machine – the Doctor sighed mightily and cursed the tiny loops which snagged up and constituted the greater part of any length of twine he'd ever head dealings with, all over the Universe. He swore he'd never leave the TARDIS again without a ball of Oombrean Snagfree 'Fine twine for thee and thine', an advertising jingle he'd coined when in a very tight spot indeed back in the Globus Wars of Independence. Well, it was the sort of thing one wrote only in very tight corners, he whimpered to himself defensively. And the rebels had needed the money . . . 'That's still no excuse,' he muttered, angrily.

'Wha'?' queried Kevin, only to be met with more frantic 'Keep it going' signals. 'Oh, right,' he sighed, 'Well, did I tell you when I came to, I was being carried by these two blokes in boiler suits? I mean they seem to use them like guards or summat around here, an' everyone wears a boiler suit. Why they can't afford a decent set of clothes beats me, I mean they didn't have my disadvantages, did they, an' I don't wear a boiler suit. Not all the time, like. I mean, not that many boilermakers carry guns, do they, not where I come from any road. Be a strike if they did, you bet your life –'

The Doctor jumped down, a broad grin on his face. 'It's all right, you can stop now.' He looked up at the video camera and made as rude a face at it as he could manage.

'I was just getting to the interesting part,' grumbled Kevin.

'Really?' replied the Doctor, unable to keep the doubt from his voice. 'Well, that should do the trick.' He gestured with manifest pride at the sonic screwdriver tied to the side of the video camera.

'Oh great,' responded Kevin flatly, 'I'd hate to think it'd all been for nothing . . . What is it?'

'That?' The Doctor shrugged modestly as he wiped his hands on one of his more florid handkerchieves. 'Oh, it's just a simple three-channel laser image loop on continuous feedback, with a quasi-random selector built into the secondary output control . . . I think.' The moment of honest doubt destroyed the effect of the bafflegab, but he didn't seem to notice . . .

'Yeah,' replied Kevin, nodding sagely, 'but what does it do?'

'Like all cameras, it lies,' replied the Doctor, shortly. 'It's sending back a picture of you, sitting on the bed, talking interminably, but in *it* I'm sitting next to you.'

'Sort of fascinated, like . . .'

'Sort of,' replied the Doctor, flinching at the thought.

'I can understand that,' Kevin said, nodding again with the wisdom of the ages, 'but why is that thing watching us anyway? I mean, this isn't your average building society or bookies, is it? I bet hardly anyone tries to knock over a place like this . . .'

'I believe it's meant to ensure that no one gets out, rather than the wrong people don't get in.'

'I know it'll take a long time, like, but whoever is watching that picture you fixed is going to smell a rat. After the first couple of days or so . . .'

'I rather think he's going to be far too distracted by whichever game he's playing with Peri –'

'What?' asked Kevin, sharply now.

'Oh, don't worry,' replied the Doctor, rather glumly though, 'that's all he does – play games . . . Calls himself the Celestial Toymaker, or did last time we met.'

'Variety act, is he?'

'That's not a bad description,' smiled the Doctor.

'And er – you. Just who are you? His agent?'

'Heaven forbid!'

'So what, then?'

'My dear chap, you'd be none the wiser if I told you in infinite detail, and it would take an awfully long time. Let's just accept things as they are, shall we, and

79

try and get out of here? Now, empty your pockets on the bed . . .'

None of which Kevin found even the slightest bit reassuring. Slowly, and watching the Doctor with great suspicion, he did as he was asked.

Three technicians in white laboratory coats stood nervously in front of the Mandarin's desk, waiting as he studied a very detailed and very complex electrical circuitry plan in front of him. Stefan stood behind them, a fact which seemed to have escaped none of them. After a long moment's consideration, the Mandarin spoke, quietly.

'The time lapse for visual response in the second phase will not be sufficient . . .'

'Exactly, Lord,' exclaimed the technician, astonished as always by the Mandarin's immediate grasp of even the most complex technical problem.

'What solution do you propose?' asked the Mandarin, gently. Too gently. The technician gulped and timidly put forward his solution.

'I believe we should increase the diameter of the carrier here, Lord –' he leaned forward and gestured to one of the hundreds of lines on the diagram – 'by not less than forty microns. That would solve the problem.'

The Mandarin studied for a moment, then beamed broadly. 'Most ingenious, Yatsumoto, thank you.' All three of the technicians joined the Mandarin in the broadest of grins, their obvious sense of relief far out of proportion to either the problem or its solution, unless you considered the Mandarin's usual penalty for failure . . . None of them knew, and never would, that the Mandarin had spotted the problem, and its solution, on first sight of the first plans. It had merely been a matter of who would spot it next, and who would solve it first. *That*, after all, was the nature of this particular game.

'Let California know the change in specification, will you?' asked the Mandarin.

'Immediately, Lord,' replied the technician and, with a small bow, all three turned and left, Stefan ushering them out. He closed the door softly. The Mandarin grinned coldly.

'You lose, Stefan.'

The henchman grinned ruefully. 'The little men are more cunning than I had realised, Lord.'

'You're not the first to notice that, I can assure you. Another hazard?'

'I can afford no more at present, Lord,' Stefan replied, with some small embarrassment.

'You'll have to win off someone else then, won't you, my boy? And soon . . .' The term 'my boy' when applied to Stefan seemed repulsive, and the glint behind the suggestion was not so much fatherly as ice-hard.

'I will, Lord,' replied Stefan, echoing the Mandarin's soft manner to convey dreadful threat.

'That, after all, is how the game is played, is it not?' The glint remained.

'Indeed, Lord.' Stefan turned to go, then stopped as he opened the door. 'Will you speak to Tokyo now, Lord? They have kept the satellite line open for some time.'

'Very well,' sighed the Mandarin and, with a wave of his hand dismissed Stefan, who closed the door quietly as he left.

The Mandarin passed a hand over his face in what was almost a human gesture of tiredness. He stood and wandered, as if aimlessly, to stand in front of a wall decorated with what was too photographic to be called a painting, too diffused to be called a photograph. Years of study by a team of the best experts on Earth might eventually deduce it was a study of a gas-cloud, though not of this or any other known galaxy, and even then, they would have no way of knowing what it meant to the Mandarin, or why he passed his hand so gently over the surface, or what thoughts passed through his head to bring a softness to his eyes which had never been seen by another living being . . .

Abruptly, he took his hand away and, almost in anger, crossed back to his desk. He sat swiftly and pressed an ivory button set into the small console there. The viewing screen immediately came to life, with a head and shoulders picture of a Japanese man, white-haired and moustached, dressed, it would seem, in a severe business suit. The eyes were watchful, though they could see only the red light on the phone camera before him, the manner calm and forceful, a manner which could only be gained by years of high office, of the habit of command. The man bowed towards the Mandarin only very slightly.

'Lord,' he greeted, his English excellent.

'Toshiro,' returned the Mandarin, a careful note in his voice.

'My board of directors is anxious for news, Lord.'

'Your board of directors is anxious when you tell them to be, Toshiro.'

'Would that were so, Lord, but alas, they are independently minded, and not so easily led as you suppose.'

'I didn't say it was easy, Toshiro, but you lead them nevertheless.'

'You are too kind, Lord.' Another small bow, but almost ironic now.

'You haven't been waiting for half an hour on satellite costs to tell me that, Toshiro. What do you want?'

'A deadline, Lord. My factories are ready –'

'So are mine, Toshiro. And the Germans, and the Americans, the Taiwanese, even the French are ready.'

'When, Lord?' It was almost a whisper.

'Soon, Toshiro.'

'I need a more definite answer than that, Lord.'

'Your needs are familiar to me, Toshiro,' replied the Mandarin, the soft tone and the hard glint never more in evidence than now. 'Profits, raw profits on a scale that only I can provide. Profits which you can join me in, but which you can never, *never* demand. Is that not so, Toshiro?'

The Japanese man's mouth tightened as the unpleasant truth was acknowledged. There was another short, sharp bow of agreement, of subservience.

'Good,' replied the Mandarin, purring. 'You may tell your . . . board . . . that the last hurdle has been overcome and that I now have the final . . . personnel . . . requirements fulfilled. The blueprints will be in your factories within the month. Is that good enough for you?'

'You are kind as you are wise, Lord,' replied Toshiro, bowing once again, and now, the Mandarin noted with amusement, there was a definite irony in the movement.

'Goodbye, Toshiro.' Without further pleasantries, the Mandarin terminated the connection. The amused smile stayed on his lips as he considered the conversation. Toshiro was an excellent player, without doubt one of the finest he'd met on this planet, but the time was coming when that particular game would reach a conclusion, a conclusion which the Japanese magnate would most certainly not enjoy, but one from which the Mandarin would wring the last drop of satisfaction. The smile broadened . . .

The Doctor looked down at the pile of flotsam and jetsam from his pockets with a fixed, almost trance-like stare. The pile was quite generous, most of it covered with fluff, ranging from a very gummy jelly baby to the signet-ring of Rasillon. An unpleasant sweetmeat to the

83

most powerful single object in the known Universes, he thought, glumly. Typical. He heaved a great sigh, for in the manner of everyone's ragtag and bobtail, every piece held a story, and there were suddenly too many memories . . . He broke off to look at Kevin's pitiful little collection, hardly able to believe his eyes.

'No transducers?' he stated, flatly. He looked up.

Kevin, seeing the look in those eyes, shook his head guiltily. Why were there no transducers in his pockets? What the hell were transducers?

'No elliptical resonators?' Again the headshake. Why oh why were there no elliptical resonators? What had he been doing with his life?

'Fuse wire?' asked the Doctor in an agony of desperation.

'It's just not the sort of stuff I carry round with me,' Kevin answered, very carefully, realising the importance of what he was saying, 'even if I knew what it was . . .'

'And look what you do carry with you!' The Doctor waved a hand in total dismissal at the little pile on the bed – a few coins, a bus ticket, a more than usually clean handkerchief. He was trying not to be too harsh, but really!

'When I was your age, I had enough "stuff" in my pockets to build a holo-field scrambler in five minutes flat, and often did!' The voice was nearing hysteria.

'Why haven't you got what you need now then?' asked Kevin in as neutral and provocative a tone as he could manage. The Doctor was about to come apart at the seams with sheer frustration, and caught himself only just in time.

'One matures . . .' he announced. He mused for a moment and then his eyes, with a sparkle, switched to the video machine in the corner. 'Can you get the back off that thing for me?'

'About thirty seconds,' nodded Kevin, matter of factly.

Stefan stood easily in front of the Mandarin's desk. The Mandarin was seated as usual, but he seemed hardly interested in the conversation, merely seeking confirmation of that which he already knew.

'When will production commence?' he asked.

'The new specification will make no difference, Lord,' replied Stefan, confidently. 'Within the month.'

'Have arrangements been made for the technicians to travel to America?'

'They leave tonight, Lord, with your permission,' he added, as a matter of course. The Mandarin nodded.

'Data correlation must be complete in two weeks, then.'

'Yes, Lord. We foresee no difficulties.'

'We could even incorporate the results from the Time Lord,' suggested the Mandarin, with an idle smile. Stefan smiled broadly.

'Then the game's appeal would be truly universal, Lord.' The Mandarin smiled again, and inclined his head in agreement. Stefan's dry unpleasant cackle filled the room.

The path Kevin had found had been winding through the ride for what seemed like miles to Peri. Sometimes it joined the layout of the mine proper, sometimes it moved back into other, disused tunnels. She supposed it must be some sort of service route, but she hoped for the maintenance crews' sakes they had a bunch of first-rate maps. They were walking on the opposite side of the railway track now, opposite a group of miners drinking what seemed to be whisky in what seemed to be a very determined fashion. Kevin paid them no attention whatsoever, whilst Peri still viewed them with the deepest suspicion. They came to a break in the path, as the ride-tracks swung away to the left to vanish into yet another tunnel, and where there was a two-step iron ladder set into the wall to take the path along a ledge and then into a tunnel of its own.

'Can't be much further now,' said Kevin as he offered her a helping hand to climb the ladder.

'How's your arm?' asked Peri casually as she took hold of his hand.

'Fine,' he replied. 'Why shouldn't it be?'

'I thought you sprained it.' He frowned briefly. 'When we escaped,' she added.

'Oh that!' He laughed quietly. 'No, it's fine now.'

'After you,' said Peri, calmly. She motioned for him to lead on, and then followed him, very carefully indeed . . .

Kevin had been true enough to his word, though perhaps a trifle optimistic, as the Doctor pointed out airily. It had taken him two minutes, not the claimed thirty seconds, but the back of the machine was now off and the Doctor was grubbing around the inside, happy as a sandboy. The business end of the machine, the long tubes designed to hold all the coins, occupied the top left quarter of the available space, and the cash boxes the bottom half. But what was left in the remaining space was a treasure chest of wiring, printed circuit boards and other electrical components, which the Doctor was busy reducing to its constituent elements.

'No, no, no,' the Doctor replied to an earlier question, 'the walls do not exist! Not that one anyway,' he modified, gesturing vaguely at the wall behind which the monster, presumably, still lurked. Kevin turned his head to look at it, and, perhaps, to make sure he had the right wall.

86

'So why does it hurt when I hit it?' he asked, reasonably enough.

'Because it's solid, of course! What d'you expect to feel when you thump a solid object? Warm all over?'

'Then if it's not real, how come I think it's there?'

'Because it is!' sighed the Doctor, exasperated, and beginning to wish he'd never embarked on this crash course in quasi-physical mechanics for beginners. 'Can't you trust the evidence of your own eyes? Or are you one of those fellows who has to go around hitting things all the time. Knew a chap like that once,' he remembered, 'in Paris . . .'

'It doesn't exist, but it's real,' Kevin recapitulated the lesson so far. 'It's not there but it's solid?'

'At last! I detect a glimmer of understanding!' Now that he seemed to have got to first base, he thought the wayward brain in front of him might stand the most basic explanation. 'It's a simple holo-field . . . like a hologram, which is just a picture made up of diffracted light, but with enough energy to give it the appearance and physical attributes of solid material – honestly, sometimes it's just like talking to primitives . . .' He poked his head out suddenly, hair awry, a sheepish look on his face. 'Sorry . . .' The head dipped back inside the machine. 'Right, that should –' Whatever he was going to say was stopped in its tracks by the sound of a key in the lock of the door. With amazing speed, and at some risk to life and limb, the Doctor was out from the back of the machine and leaning nonchalantly against it by the time the door opened and the ancient Shardlow came in, bearing a large tray. The two boiler suits accompanying him stayed outside, and made no attempt to help.

With a gentle bow to the Doctor, Shardlow bore the tray over to the rough table and started to lay out a fine service of plates, cutlery, thick damask napkins, then bowls of soup, bread rolls and pâté.

'My apologies for the victuals, masters,' he spoke softly, 'cook was expecting you much earlier and does not, alas, reside in the house.'

'Who are you?' asked Kevin, not unkindly.

'My name is Shardlow, sir.'

'What do you do here, Shardlow?'

'I am a servant here, sir, as are we all in our own way . . .'

'Why do you stay here,' demanded Kevin, 'in this madhouse?'

'Is there a choice, young sir?' asked the old man, matter-of-factly.

The Doctor went up to him. 'Which game did you lose at, Shardlow?' he asked, as gently as he could.

'Why, backgammon, sir. At the Hellfire Club, it was. A losing hazard . . .' He smiled ruefully at the memory.

'And when was this?' the Doctor asked, even more gently.

'Why, a beautiful summer's evening, sir. The July of '78.'

'Ten years?' queried Kevin, horrified. 'In this dump!' The Doctor looked at him, sadly, then turned back to the old man.

'You mean 1778, don't you, old chap?'

'Why yes, sir,' replied Shardlow, obviously surprised there should be any confusion.

'That's over two hundred years ago!' exclaimed Kevin.

'Is it, master? Is it indeed? I must confess, it has sometimes seemed such a very long time . . .' The wistfulness in the old man's voice stopped even Kevin from further protest, and one of the boiler suits came towards the cell as if to see what all the chatter was about. Shardlow was the first to notice, and raised his voice immediately.

'I will return, good sirs, in a quarter of an hour, with the fish course. Sadly, we do not keep as fine a table these days as once we did.'

'Times change, Shardlow,' said the Doctor, softly.

'Do they, sir? Do they indeed?'

Slowly and sadly, the old man limped out and the sound of the key was heard in the door again.

'This place is nuthin' but a flamin' asylum,' insisted Kevin. 'I've never heard such a load of complete codswallop in all me born days!'

'What you've just heard is the plain, unvarnished truth, I should think,' replied the Doctor sombrely.

'Two-hundred-year-old geezers serving the grub?'

'More than two hundred,' the Doctor pointed out. 'That's just the time he's been here – he was his natural age before that – say, what – sixty?'

'Oh, that makes a lot more sense that does,' snorted Kevin, 'him being two hundred and sixty instead of two hundred. That makes it a lot more credible!'

'That poor old man,' murmured the Doctor, turning to look after the way Shardlow had gone. 'The gift of immortality didn't seem to please him that much, did it?'

'Immortality?' asked Kevin, unused to such concepts as facts of life.

'When you can start counting your age in centuries, you can call that immortality, can't you? Of a sort?' The mood of melancholy seemed to change abruptly, as reaction set in to what he had just witnessed. 'Or like the rest of your race, are you going to quibble about definitions?'

Kevin was somewhat taken aback, sensing that the Doctor was not having a dig at the Anglo-Saxons, but rather the whole polyglot of Homo Sapiens in general.

'Yes, that would be typical,' continued the Doctor, working up a good head of steam now, 'to spend the rest of eternity defining immortality – that would really satisfy the human race's yearning for self-justification! That poor old man . . .' He stopped and shook his head again, compassion almost overwhelming him. 'Centuries of servitude, slavery for what? Losing at a board game! And the game would have been rigged as well! This time the Toymaker has gone too far.'

There was a grimness in his tone which Kevin had certainly never heard before, and he resolved for the foreseeable future to keep his smart remarks to himself, and pity anyone else who got in the way of his cell-mate while he was in this mood. And this mood didn't look as though it would go away until the old man, as well as themselves, was free and clear of the lunatic in charge of this particular asylum.

'This time the Toymaker has gone too far . . .'

As the words of the Doctor echoed through his consciousness, the Mandarin clapped his hands with glee, 'Excellent, excellent.'

He related the Time Lord's outburst to Stefan who advanced, his face, never the most reposed visage, now a mask of fury. 'I will have him impaled, Lord. His ending will be a terrible lesson to all, echoing down the ages.'

'Oh, you're very harsh, Stefan,' sighed the Mandarin with affected dismay. He hardened as he continued, 'I should then find it even more difficult engaging the interest of competitors, shouldn't I?' This seemed to present no decent argument to Stefan, who was quite used to his opponents playing at the point of a gun. 'The old man served his purpose very well,' continued the Mandarin. 'The Doctor's righteous indignation will raise the adrenalin level to a far more combative level.' He grinned hugely and turned the crystal ball until Peri and Kevin swam into view once more. Still grinning, he leaned forward slightly towards the screen and breathed, 'We must hurry.'

'We must hurry . . .' said Kevin, a note of urgency creeping into his voice.

'Why?' asked Peri.

'Why?' repeated Kevin, dumbly.

'I mean, why now, especially?' She had stopped to ask Kevin the question and, from the corner of her eye, watched another boiler suit duck behind some cover. They had been following them, she knew, for the last half-hour at least. And if she had seen them, Kevin must have seen them too. 'What was the deal?' she asked, off-handedly.

'What?' repeated Kevin.

'When you sold out,' she continued. 'Your brother back, was that it?'

'I don't understand,' started Kevin, feebly.

Peri hefted the crowbar. 'Stay back,' she warned, as he moved towards her. But Kevin chose to ignore the warning and made a dive for her. With all the pent-up tension and plain anger of the last couple of hours, she brought it round in a terrific belt, half-expecting his head to fly off in the same way the miner's had done, back in the ride. Instead the crowbar simply whooshed through the head as if it wasn't there. The arm which came up to catch hers was real enough though, and it held her long enough for the boiler suits to come running up and hold her even more securely. Kevin stepped back, and surveyed the girl with disdain.

'The start of the game was most amusing, and I wish I could say you were a worthy opponent,' he sneered, 'but in truth, you need to practise for a very long time. We shall have to see what we can do about that.'

'Who are you?' Peri whispered, but the figure of Kevin merely laughed, thinly and without humour. Then the figure started to shimmer and, with no sound at all, faded away. The two guards seemed not at all surprised by the effect, as they led Peri, unprotesting, away.

Chapter Seven

Tearing off another great lump of the delicious bread rolls, Kevin waved the remainder at the Doctor and pronounced, in his flat, atonal Liverpudlian voice, a thought that had been building in his brain for several minutes now. 'You could use that very nicely to strain broccoli, you know. Patent it and make a fortune. I'm very fond of a bit of broccoli, but it's the very devil to strain.'

'Unlike what passes for your brain,' muttered the Doctor. He gave a yank and another clump of wire came out of the back of the video game machine, and, industriously, he started plaiting that into the dish shape he had already fashioned, convex with an antennae device at the centre, concentric circles of wire held apart by radials, producing the effect of a circular spider's web, or, if you prefer, a perfect broccoli strainer.

'But I reckon you're goin' to use it for somethin' else,' Kevin added, sagaciously.

'Going to have to, old chap,' admitted the Doctor frankly. Kevin looked mildly surprised. 'No broccoli,' explained the Doctor, and disappeared into the innards of the machine again. Kevin looked thoughtful as he bit into his bread roll again. Where could he get some broccoli?

'The technicians await your pleasure, Lord,' announced Stefan, waiting at the door. The Mandarin turned from his thoughts, a broad smile still on his face.

93

'Stefan, I have just been busy enjoying myself, a feeling I haven't had for a very long time. A very long time indeed.'

'I am glad to hear it, Lord,' replied Stefan, unsurely. The Mandarin's idea of enjoyment was rarely Stefan's – or anyone else's for that matter – and Stefan was wisely reluctant to commit himself until he knew more about the nasty little pleasure the Mandarin had devised for himself now. Given the time the Mandarin seemed prepared to devote to even the simplest diversion, it had to be grotesque indeed.

'You don't understand, Stefan,' said the Mandarin, giving voice to a thought that had occurred to him a hundred times a day for longer than even he cared to remember. 'I have actually found a distraction . . . something I can even develop. Something with almost boundless possibilities – why, it could be good for centuries yet. I cannot become another person – that is beyond even my capabilities – but I can *pretend* to be another person, to the point where even his dearest friend or closest relative would never know the difference – the possibilities for sport are positively enormous.' The glee in his voice made even Stefan shudder. He had seen the Mandarin at work for long enough now to be passingly familiar with his caprices – was he not here now through just those caprices? 'I owe that young lady and her friend a great deal,' he finished, dreamily.

Stefan summoned up the courage to take advantage of what seemed to be the Mandarin's good humour. 'Lord, may I proceed with my game of backgammon – the old man . . .?' he prompted, as he saw the momentary puzzlement in the Mandarin's eyes.

As he placed the request in context, the Mandarin answered, testily, 'Yes, yes, after the trial run, if you wish . . .' and dismissed him with a wave of his hand.

Stefan grinned with anticipated satisfaction and turned to go, but was pulled up short as the Mandarin called after him, softly, 'But, Stefan, make sure *you* win, won't you?'

He grinned evilly at the discomfort on his henchman's face, and Stefan swallowed hard before he muttered his reply, 'Yes, Lord . . .'

In the Mandarin's realm, there was always an unpleasant price for failure, however small. Always unpleasant . . .

The Doctor stared broodily at the dish-shaped antennae. 'You sure you haven't got any transducers?'

Kevin shook his head anxiously, without looking through his pockets. He felt sure he would know if he *had* got any transducers, even if he didn't know a transducer from a muddy hole in the ground. The Doctor made a face at the antennae.

'Won't it work without one?' asked Kevin, more to ease the silence than in a genuine search for technical knowledge.

'Of course it won't work without one,' snapped the Doctor. 'How could it possibly work without one? D'you think I'd be sitting here twiddling my technically brilliant thumbs if it would work without one? It might . . . it just might . . .' he finished, muttering to himself, but the thought was overtaken by the sound of bootsteps in the corridor, and he had only just enough time to stuff the antennae under the bed as Kevin pushed the machine back to the wall before there was the sound of the key in the lock and Peri was pushed without ceremony into the cell.

'You didn't last long,' greeted the Doctor, never one for over-sentimentalising. The door slammed behind her before she could protest at her rude treatment, and the Doctor had jumped up on the bed and was

95

fiddling with the sonic-screwdriver attachment to the surveillance camera before she could upbraid him about his compassionate welcome.

'What are you doing?' she asked instead.

'Just putting you in the picture,' he replied, pleasantly. He finished and jumped down again, dusting off his hands. 'Easier with practice,' he announced, smugly.

'What do'you mean "didn't last long"? I was nearly killed out there, so was he.' She pointed at Kevin. 'Both of him . . .'

'A copy?' queried the Doctor.

'What d'you mean, "both of me"?' asked Kevin, a split second behind.

'Not a physical copy,' explained Peri to the Doctor. 'Well, he was to start with but then he just – faded away . . .'

'Like the door,' pronounced the Doctor, nodding his head.

'He was not like a door,' protested Peri.

'Simple hologram, that's all,' shrugged Kevin. The Doctor beamed and nodded and then bent to retrieve the antennae from under the bed. Kevin took the opportunity to point an exaggerated finger at him, indicating more clearly than any words 'Humour him . . .'

'Solid, but not real, you know.' He nodded at Peri vigorously, who was forced to agree with him.

'Yeah, sure, that's the idea . . .'

The Doctor straightened slowly, the antennae in hand and turned to look at Kevin.

'Solid but not real,' he repeated.

'Yeah, right on. That's the stuff, yeah.'

The Doctor continued to look at him critically. 'Doesn't exist, but it's there . . .'

'That's it, that's exactly right. Couldn't have put it better meself,' replied Kevin, encouragingly.

The Doctor continued to look at him and then reached up and tweaked his ear. Hard.

'Awk!' screeched Kevin. 'That hurt, that did –'

'Seems real enough to me,' shrugged the Doctor to Peri, 'but then you never can tell with holograms. That's the point really, isn't it?' He smiled pleasantly, as he moved over to the machine and pulled it back from the wall again.

'Here, just a minute,' twigged Kevin, 'you think I'm a . . . hologram.'

'Not any more,' grinned Peri.

'Does he do that to you?' Kevin asked her, rubbing his ear.

'Not any more,' she and the Doctor replied in unison, he from the bowels of the machine.

'Known each other long, have you?' Kevin asked, looking at her with as much suspicion as the Doctor had previously regarded him.

'Yes,' replied Peri, shortly.

'Long enough to give me a hand?' called the Doctor from inside the machine. She grinned and went over to bend down by him. Immediately there was a puff of smoke and a coughing, slightly smudged Doctor appeared.

'You are back, aren't you? Now look what you've made me do . . .'

There was only one change in the data room, but it was a major one. The tables and chairs which had been at the centre of the room had been taken out, and whilst the computers still clicked away tirelessly, pride of place was given to an enormous video games machine – seven feet tall, as wide as two ordinary machines, with a huge screen, curving almost from over the head off the player back to its base. The effect created was that of a head-up display which might be

97

found on a very sophisticated space shuttle, or a very basic starship.

The machine breathed shiny and new at everyone who looked at it, and many were looking at it at the moment. All the senior staff of the Mandarin's several establishments were there – a dozen and a half of the finest technological brains in the industry, all in their white coats, all waiting . . . The low murmur of conversation died and floated away as Stefan heralded the entrance of the Mandarin, who crossed straight to the machine and looked at it with fatherly pride.

'Beautiful,' he breathed, 'beautiful . . .' There were congratulatory smiles all round. 'All is well?' he asked of the assembled company. Yatsumoto spoke for all.

'The prototype performs perfectly, Lord.' He smiled with smug satisfaction.

'You've tried it?' queried the Mandarin with polite surprise.

'In its component parts, honoured Lord,' modified the technician, 'there is no error –'

'But you haven't actually *played* the machine?' The Mandarin's insistence on an exact answer was no whim.

'I understood that honour was to be reserved for your esteemed guest – ' Yatsumoto looked around him, unsure of his master's mood.

'To the victor, the spoils, Yatsumoto. You shall be the first to play.' He started applauding softly, and the rest of the assembly joined in. Yatsumoto looked suitably flattered, but as much confused as anything. He could hardly refuse, and had yet to come across the western term 'poisoned chalice' in any of his technical manuals, but he sensed there was something wrong, some hidden purpose in the Mandarin's offer. Why else the shudder of fear as he approached the shiny new toy?

*

The Doctor was sitting on the floor, cross-legged, one tangle of wires over one shoulder, one over the other as he weaved them together in an intricate pattern which seemed to owe more to rope-making than electronics. One end of the electrical rope was attached to the back of the machine, one end to the antennae, and when he had finished this stretch, the circuit would be complete.

'. . . I don't know who he is,' he answered Peri's question as simply as he could. 'Nobody knows. He existed before the start of Time Lord records. There was an attempt to track him back through his own continuum – trace his path through the fabric of time, but the researchers got bored with all the games, which was possibly what they were there for. As they do so often,' he sighed, 'my erstwhile colleagues met something they didn't understand, and they ran away from it. If they'd been able to control him, they would have investigated further, I'm sure. But they couldn't, so they didn't.'

'A being the Time Lords couldn't handle?' asked Peri with a worried frown.

'Oh, there are plenty of *them*,' the Doctor reassured her. 'Time Lords generally aren't very good at handling things, especially themselves. I'm just the exception to the rule.'

'Right,' answered Peri. She wasn't going to argue with that last remark under any circumstances.

On a more positive note, the Doctor continued: 'We know he's telepathic, up to a point. We know he's telekinetic, up to a point. We know he can stand the most violent physical forces in our experience – he was once observed playing with a supernova as though it was a kiddies' paddling pool . . . and we know he's old beyond imagining . . .' The comment seemed to distract him for a moment, but then he shook himself and continued. 'Most of all, we know he likes games, all sorts of games, any sort of games, and the nastier the better. And that's what I'm going to do something about.' He was as quietly determined as Peri had ever seen him. It was left to Kevin to voice the sceptical question.

'You're going to beat him, then?'

'I'm going to escape from him,' answered the Doctor, coldly, 'and count myself very lucky if I do even that.'

The conversation was once again cut short by the sound of approaching footsteps in the corridor, but by now the team had a routine as they camouflaged the electronic work, pushed the video game machine back to the wall and busied themselves looking as innocently inactive as prisoners should. By the time the door opened to admit Shardlow once more, they looked as though they'd been sitting there for years.

'My apologies for the delay, masters.'

'Nonsense, my dear fellow, we were just remarking on the speed and excellence of the service, weren't we, chaps?' the Doctor replied, jovially. There was a thoroughly unenthusiastic agreement from Kevin, and a wan smile from Peri. 'If only the accommodation were in the same style, eh?'

Shardlow looked both concerned and worried. 'Alas, sir, my Lord has instructed you be kept close confined.'

'I didn't think this was all your idea, old chap,' replied the Doctor, drily. Shardlow looked relieved.

'Indeed not, sir.' He turned to Peri. 'Mistress, I took the liberty of bringing a portion for you also.'

'Thank you.'

Shardlow bent to his task of serving them from an oval platter – a delicious smelling fish dish in a cream and mushroom sauce. He carried on clearing away the dirty soup dishes as his eye caught sight of the antennae, hidden under the bed not quite as well as it should have been. He addressed his next remarks with heavy emphasis to the Doctor, looking him straight in the eye all the while.

'Unfortunately, both my Lord and the Master Stefan are much engaged by the Great Work, to the exclusion of all else. They have little time to devote to your good selves, I fear. Not so much as they would like, I know. In a short time, however, I am sure they will be able to concern themselves entirely with you, and will take much pleasure in so doing . . .'

'Thank you, Shardlow,' replied the Doctor, quietly. 'I appreciate your consideration.'

Shardlow inclined his head in acknowledgement, and allowed a gentle smile to reach his lips for a moment only. Peri was starting to catch on, but Kevin had missed the code entirely, breaking into the moment abruptly with the question uppermost in his mind.

'Here, is there anyone else in this place like us?' Shardlow was about to reply, but Kevin rushed on regardless. 'I mean, you know – anyone halfway normal. Anyone playing with a full deck of cards?' Again Shardlow was about to speak, but Kevin was determined to get it out. 'For instance a bloke a bit like me only younger, four years younger actually, dark hair, quite tall, not as good-lookin'. Goes by the name of Geoff Bickerstaff . . .' He paused, as if daring Shardlow to reply.

'Why yes, young sir,' replied Shardlow, unable to keep the note of surprise from his voice, 'Master Bickerstaff to be sure, but he is not like you at all – that is to say – I mean no –'

'What? What's the matter? Is he all right?'

'Why yes, sir. But Master Bickerstaff is an honoured guest of My Lord, his trusted assistant in the Great Work . . .'

★

101

The screen on the game machine was filled with a three-dimensional block outline of a city – an American city, judging by the skyscrapers – in wonderful detail. It seemed that the player could control his movement down the street by use of the control joystick in front of him. The city was deserted. As Yatsumoto directed himself around a corner, a burning car could be seen, smashed into another at the side of the street. Broken windows were everywhere, and the goods scattered on the pavement seemed to indicate a riot, or looting at any rate. As Yatsumoto drew nearer to the crashed cars, a heavy *crunchcrunchcrunch* noise started, and grew louder.

From behind one of the crashed cars a figure appeared, a green, or red, glowing figure, it was hard to tell which as it kept changing colour back and forth. As Yatsumoto moved towards the figure, so the figure moved towards him, then there was an arc of fire and a sound effect as Yatsumoto fired his weaponry. The figure glowed bright red and swelled and burst into a million electronic fragments. Yatsumoto grinned broadly, ignoring the sweat trickling down his forehead. The score counter at the top of the screen flickered, registering the kill but, before he had time to gloat, the *crunchcrunch* noise started again, and another figure appeared from behind the burning car and lines of fire came at *him*, so effectively that he flinched. The screen lit up and jarred, and jarred again. This time he did flinch – it was impossible not to, and with the third shock registering on the screen, he couldn't help looking at the Lives on the bottom line. He had started off with three. Now there were two . . .

Grimly he set his mouth, and concentrated as the screen changed to show another part of the city. Yatsumoto did not look at all pleased. He was back at the start, and with one life less.

★

'Assistant?' queried Kevin, unbelieving.

'Great Work?' asked the Doctor, believing all too completely.

'Why, mercy yes, my masters. For what other purpose must we all serve?' The Doctor was about to tell him, and in no uncertain terms, but the old man carried on, dreamily. 'Not that I shall see the fruits of my labours . . . Master Stefan has called me to a game of backgammon, and I shall lose. I always do lose,' he added, without any rancour at all, 'but I am promised that this is to be the last game.' There was the faintest note of wistfulness in his voice, but then he turned to the Doctor and continued far more surely. 'And I believe I owe you a great debt of thanks, noble sir.

'Do you?'

'Why yes, sir. Master Stefan said directly that now you had arrived to help our Lord, the Work would soon be completed. And thus my last game has come.'

'And what is the hazard this time, Shardlow?' The Doctor asked, grimly, although he believed he already knew the answer.

'Why, sir,' answered Shardlow with a soft smile, 'what else does an old man have to wager?' The Doctor nodded heavily. Peri saw it in a flash of understanding.

'Your *life*?'

'Of a certainty, mistress.' There was even a soft chuckle. 'And Master Stefan has always been one to call in a wager. For once, I cannot lose, for even in losing, I shall win my freedom. Is that not so?'

The Doctor nodded again in agreement, and extended his hand. 'Good fortune in any case, Shardlow. Give him a run for his money.'

'Thank you sir, I believe I shall.' He took the Doctor's hand gladly, 'Yes, tonight, I believe I shall.'

★

Yatsumoto was perspiring freely now, his hands at the controls tense and never still as he approached the burning cars once more. The *crunchcrunch* started again and, sure enough, the figure came out again, and sure enough met the same fate. This time Yatsumoto waited grimly for the second figure to show, and finished him off when he did. Then he poured fire into the blazing cars for good measure, and sure enough a third figure leapt out, only to disappear in a constellation of exploding sparks . . . Nodding with satisfaction, the Japanese technician moved himself further along the street and around the corner to be met instantly by a deafening *crunchcrunch* and a red and green monster, almost upon him. There was a blaze of fire arcing towards him, the screen flashed one, two, three times, and he almost slumped at the controls.

The Lives indicator went down by one again. Yatsumoto wiped the palms of his hands down his laboratory coat. Only one life left.

Peri was sitting on the bed, glumly holding the antennae as the Doctor worked behind the games machine.

'That poor old man,' she said sadly, unknowingly echoing the Doctor's earlier sentiments.

'He'll be all right,' reassured Kevin.

'Depends what you mean by "all right",' muttered the Doctor from the bowels of the machine.

'Well, they wouldn't hurt him, would they? Not over a stupid game.'

'If he loses, I shouldn't think he'll feel a thing,' said the Doctor in his matter-of-fact voice. 'We'll just have to get there before the game's over, that's all.' His face appeared from behind the machine for a moment. 'Give me a fork, would you?' Kevin reached one from the food tray and made to pass it to him. 'A *clean* one,' asked the Doctor with a note of exasperation. Kevin hunted through the discarded cutlery, and came up with an unused fork. 'What did you train as,' grumbled the Doctor, taking it suspiciously, 'a plumber's mate?' But before Kevin could reply effectively, he had disappeared down his electronic warren again.

Yatsumoto was firing indiscriminately now, monsters exploding thick and fast around every corner. The *crunchcrunch* was everywhere, sometimes just in the background, sometimes almost next to his ear.

The lines of fire suddenly stopped arcing from his weaponry. Frantically he jabbed at the Fire button on the joystick and then he looked at the ammunition counter, a red line at the side of the screen with little green lines sticking up from it. There were no little green lines left.

From the left and the right, monsters appeared, firing as they did so. The ghost city was ablaze with gunfire and the *crunchcrunch* of approaching monsters. The lines of fire raced towards him, a hit, a hit, another hit . . . The screen flashed for the last time, and the monsters faded away, the noise receding to a distant but insistent *crunchcrunchcrunch*.

Yatsumoto looked shattered, slumped at the controls. Then his attention was engaged as the *crunchcrunch* became louder and louder. He looked puzzled, then bewildered. The game was over. He had lost. He had been playing under field-trial conditions, just as people would be soon, all over the world. The Mandarin smiled, the glint back in his eye. The *crunchcrunch* became louder and louder.

From the centre of the screen, lumbering down the street, came one of the electronic monsters, though no firing took place. The figure walked towards Yatsumoto, growing in size as he came.

Growing. And growing. And growing.

Yatsumoto stepped back from the machine instinctively. The monster filled the screen. More than filled it.

'Lord . . . Stop it, Lord, I beg you . . .'

The Mandarin watched, fascinated to see it all *working*.

The monster stepped *out* from the screen.

It grew before his eyes, reaching seven feet tall, thick set and heavily built on legs that were almost too squat for the enormous body, a body composed entirely of red and green crystals, hard, flat, angular surfaces like cut gemstones, with two giant burning red rubies for eyes, and no other facial features at all.

It stood in the room, waiting. The other technicians had moved back as far as they could go and now stood also, terrified and horrified by the apparition. The monster moved its head and stood, staring balefully at Yatsumoto.

'Help me, Lord . . . *Save me!*' he screamed at the Mandarin.

'But you lost, Yatsumoto,' called the Mandarin over the rising *crunchcrunchcrunch*. 'You *lost.*'

The monster turned and, implacably, advanced on Yatsumoto, who had nowhere to run. He backed up against a laboratory bench, head pressed back against one of his beloved computers. The monster advanced. The *crunchcrunch* became unbearable and Yatsumoto thrust his hands over his ears, as if by cutting out the sound he could make the monster go away.

But the monster stopped in front of him and, almost responding in kind, placed one of its giant hands on either side of Yatsumoto's head. With some enormous discharge, a red electric arc leapt between the two hands and Yatsumoto's body glowed red and green like the monster's, then black and white as it went from positive to negative and back again. Then the hands came away

106

and Yatsumoto slumped to the ground heavily, his coat smoking slightly where it touched the ground. The monster stood stockstill and the *crunchcrunchcrunch* faded away to nothing. The Mandarin came over to look and admire.

'What a *marvellous* toy,' he breathed.

Peri had been waiting, eyes squeezed almost shut, for what seemed like most of her life. The antennae were pointed squarely at the cell door, as the Doctor had instructed, the umbilical cord of the knitted cable running back to the game machine. The Doctor had told her to 'stand by' half a dozen times, and after each occasion had muttered some variation on the 'hang on a tick' theme, and then rushed to make some adjustment to the electronics. He was behind the machine now, and her confidence in this very Heath Robinson affair was dwindling like sand through her fingers. A triumphant cry from him jerked her eyes open and Kevin, not at all reassuringly, pulled another pillow from the bed over his head.

'Right,' called the Doctor, and evidently switched on, for a heavy humming started from the machine, and seemed to run along the cable and resonate through the antennae Peri was holding, so much so that she nearly dropped it. She was about to call out in distress when, to her and everyone else's astonishment, it worked. The door started to disappear.

The Doctor let out a great 'Yarroo' of success; even Kevin let out an 'and about time too' sort of approbation, which immediately turned to a groan. Peri turned her head to see what Kevin and the Doctor were staring at.

As the door had started to disappear, so had the right-hand cell wall, revealing the claw-waving spider crab. So had the left-hand cell wall, revealing a shimmering

107

electronic mass of sickly pink, held in a vaguely dog-like shape. So had the back cell wall, revealing a half man, half robot dressed head to foot in black, with only half a human face.

Peri screamed and dropped the antennae, which had no effect on the advancing monsters. Kevin sprang up with a clatter as the table bearing the food tray went over, which had even less effect. The Doctor could only stand, stunned, as the monsters moved towards him . . .

Chapter Eight

The technicians in the data room were silent now. They knelt on one knee, bowed in homage to their Lord. The Mandarin drank it all in, the glint still in his eye as he surveyed them. The monster stood, motionless, massive, in the centre of the room, next to the deadly video game that had spawned it. In a modest voice belied by his imperial manner, the Mandarin spoke:

'Come now, no need for that, we aren't in the Dark Ages now, not for a while anyway.' He smiled and gestured for them to rise. 'But the time is coming,' he added softly, too softly for any but Stefan to hear. 'The time is coming . . .'

Stefan grinned his wolfish grin.

The three of them were squeezed into a huddle now as the monsters advanced upon them, until the Doctor, recovering from the trance into which his unexpected results in elecronic engineering had sent them, sprang up on the bed to rattle away on the pipe again. The Claw wavered, and then stopped. The man-robot hesitated. The pink cloud melted back to its former position.

'It's all right,' called the Doctor to his companions. 'There's no reason to suppose they want to hurt us.'

Kevin and Peri looked at the Claw, and at the robot – clad, it seemed, half in armour – and at the manic pink cloud, then wondered what particular train of logic lead the Doctor to *that* conclusion.

The android started to move forward again. 'I say, you sound to me like a sort of sentient thing?'

The rich plummy accent of perfect English spun the Doctor round from an initial appraisal of the door. 'Sort of,' he replied, shortly.

'Oh, good show,' chortled the android. 'Very good show. Getting a bit lonely down here, tell the truth.' In the absence of any response from the Doctor, who tested the door by sticking his finger into the opening, and then pulled it back as he stung it on the invisible barrier again, the android paused for a moment or two, and then spoke again, much louder and much more slowly. 'You know "lonely"?'

'Yes, I know "lonely",' aped the Doctor. 'What d'you think I am, an unfeeling block?' As if to demonstrate the reverse, he continued alternately sucking and shaking his finger until the stinging went away.

'Eh?' replied the android, uncomprehendingly.

'And I'm not a foreigner,' added the Doctor, crossly. 'You don't have to shout.'

'Oh right, yes, sorry,' shuffled the man-robot, with what would have been a self-conscious grin on his face, if he'd had a proper face.

'Tourists!' muttered the Doctor.

The Mandarin watched idly as the technician's assistants cleared away the debris of the previous game in much the same way as the Caesars must have watched the bestiarii clear up after the lions.

'After tonight,' he relayed to Stefan, 'I think we should move to our centre of production. There really is too much distraction here, and it's possible that we may soon attract the attention of the local militia . . . America, in any case, will be the best place to watch the Great Game.'

'I will make the necessary arrangements,' muttered Stefan. He half-bowed and made to go, but stopped short as he realised that to skirt round the Mandarin and make for the door would lead him perilously close to the electronic monster.

'Afraid, Stefan?' he taunted mildly. 'You?'

'A man would be foolish to fight that which he cannot kill,' muttered the henchman, darkly, eyeing the monster with a mixture of fear and admiration.

'Very wise, Stefan,' taunted the Mandarin again, pleased at the further demonstration of a lesson well learned. Now to press it home further . . . He crossed to the electronic monster and, taking care not to touch it, reached up and placed a hand on either side of the monster's head. He closed his eyes, and the ignorant would have assumed he was saying his prayer. Stefan was ignorant . . . A thin blue spark ran between his hands, passing through the monster's head. In much the same way as the cell door had, but much more quickly, the monster faded away and was gone into nothingness. Stefan's eyes widened to black, staring pools.

'You need be afraid of nothing of which you are the master, Stefan.'

'No, Lord,' replied the henchman, hoarsely, as he bowed his head sharply until his chin touched his chest, and the Mandarin was left in no doubt whatsoever as to who was Master in Stefan's eyes. He positively gleamed with satisfaction.

'Sort of boffin bloke, are you?' asked the android, squinting over the Doctor's shoulder at the antennae he was holding in a markedly disgruntled fashion.

'I'm not a sort of anything,' replied the Doctor irritably, and unfairly, for he had referred to himself as a sort of something ever since he'd had to start explaining his presence almost anywhere he'd visited during several lifetimes tootling around the Universe. 'We haven't been introduced,' he announced, accusingly.

111

'Oh, so sorry,' replied the android. 'One forgets the courtesies, out here on the frontier.' He stood smartly to attention, eyes staring straight ahead as he barked out, 'SB5496 oblique 74, at your service, sir.'

'SB?' queried the Doctor.

'Yes?' queried back the android.

'What does that stand for?'

'Stand for? Curious idea. Doesn't stand for anything. It's my name.' The creature seemed both puzzled, and now worried, as though the Doctor's question had touched some deep and hidden insecurity.

Blithely unaware of the psychological shock waves breaking around him, the Doctor introduced himself. 'I'm the Doctor, and this is Peri, and this is Kevin.' They all shook hands, SB still with some self-consciousness. The Doctor turned towards the Claw. 'And this is, er' he waved his hand vaguely in the air 'this is – well, I can't get my tongue around his name, all glottal stops and consonants, sort of Cockney Welsh, terrible language –'

'Oh, we just call him Mechanic,' explained SB cheerfully.

'Very imaginative,' replied the Doctor, drily.

'Why?' asked Peri in all innocence.

'Turns out he's a Ventusan,' explained the Doctor, wiping hands on a now rather florid and rather grubby handkerchief. 'They fix things. All the time. Everywhere. Anything from a washing machine to a starship engine. They run half the spacefleets in the galaxy, or rather,' he added very pedantically, 'they keep half the spacefleets in the galaxy running.' He looked at SB to appreciate the niceties of the distinction. 'There is a difference, is there not?'

'Oh, they fix things all right,' agreed SB. Which was about as much sagacious wit as the Doctor could look

112

for in that direction. 'Charge the apogee for it, though,' he muttered, darkly.

'Well, what d'you expect?' snapped the Doctor. 'It's the only thing they *can* do –'

The lesson in macro-economics also seemed to float wistfully, lost and forgotten over SB's head. 'Funny thing, evolution,' he mused, the half metal head threatening to cave in under the stress of the mental effort required to produce the thought.

'A fellow philosopher!' cried the Doctor, his intellectual snobbery rising unbidden to the surface. 'How refreshing! And who's our shimmering friend in the corner?' He gestured at the pink cloud, who had lost his almost-doggy shape now and was more in the way of a three-legged giraffe, engaged in the laborious process, it seemed, of growing a second head.

' 'Fraid I don't know, old chap,' apologised SB. 'We did meet at a shooting match upstairs – that's my game, really, shooting things,' he confided to the assembly in general, but Peri in particular. 'But the Toymaker fellah, he made some remark about the number of angels dancing on the head of a pin . . . I'm sure it was angels,' he added, worried again, 'and that thing went into meditation like a shot. Been there ever since. About, oh, seven years now, I suppose.'

The Doctor suddenly remembered. 'You must be part of the pangalactic Second Federation Force for Peace.'

'Third Federation, actually, old chap,' SB explained, again apologetically. 'Bit of a brouhaha with the second . . . Revolutionaries, fifth column . . . loyal opposition. Something along those lines, anyway. That's when the fourth front opened up, and that's when the old pins went, too.' He smacked his tin legs cheerfully, and beamed at them all in pride and joy.

'You're a scout, then?' surmised the Doctor.

113

'Rather. Call ourselves Pathfinders, now.'

'And you had a famous tradition, as I recall . . .'

'We always get our man, yes, that's it. That's the old Pathfinder tradition. Never lost one yet.'

The Doctor turned to Peri. 'The Scouts are always followed by their base support teams. Anything happens to one of them, the battle group follows up and –'

'Knocks seven colours of ichor out of the opposition,' chortled SB. 'Shoot first, ask questions after. Not that there's ever been anyone to question. Nothing but nuclear waste for parsecs,' he added, obviously very gratified at the thought. 'Good old Pathfinders . . .'

'And poor old Earth,' muttered the Doctor.

'How much of you is – actually . . . original?' asked Peri, with a delicate hesitancy.

'Left hand,' replied SB, proudly, 'oh, and a bit of my ear,' he added, touching the appendage fondly.

'Our heroic friend here has been engaged in the most futile interplanetary war in modern history for about – a hundred and eighty, hundred and ninety years now?' The Doctor looked to SB for confirmation.

'Had our bicentennial celebrations just before I left,' confided SB. 'Jolly good show, what?'

'But, don't you mind?' asked Peri, pityingly.

'Mind? Sorry, don't follow . . .'

Peri was about to gesture at what remained of his *corpus delicti* when the Doctor tried to explain the other fellow's point of view.

'*Dulce et decorum est pro patria mori.*'

'No, no, sorry,' returned SB blankly, mouth slackening as he admitted total defeat in following even the slightest thread of the conversation.

'It is a sweet and becoming thing to die for one's country,' translated the Doctor, with distinct distaste.

SB's eyes misted over. 'Oh, I say, that's beautiful. You – you feel that way too, do you? Damn good.'

He looked as though he was about to choke up and embrace the Doctor in a thoroughly manly fashion, but the Doctor had already covered his eyes in exasperation and sat heavily on the bed. He looked at their new companions with something less than enthusiasm.

'A gung-ho robot, a ravenous space plumber and a transcendental pink cloud,' he muttered. 'We're going to make an unbeatable combination . . .'

'All is prepared, Lord,' announced Stefan, as he entered the data room and crossed to the Mandarin's side. The room had indeed been returned to its former orderly status, and only one or two of the technicians were tending the machines.

'Good,' approved the Mandarin, shortly. He delicately beckoned Stefan a little closer. 'When the final phase is completed tonight, we shall have to reconsider our . . . employment policy. Those who do not accompany us to America . . .'

'I beg you, do not concern yourself with details, Lord,' replied Stefan, softly. 'Their contracts of employment will be properly . . . terminated.'

The Mandarin beamed. 'Excellent, Stefan. I knew I could rely on your . . . discretion.'

'Always, Lord.' He bowed his head in homage once again.

'Go now,' instructed the Mandarin. 'Anticipation might be half the pleasure, but I have waited long enough. Bring the Doctor to me. We shall play a game, he and I . . .'

The Doctor continued tapping out his message, nutcrackers in hand, but now using the metal bedstead as his transmitter. The Claw replied with what sounded like hysterical snapping of his mandible, tied in with a

115

couple of bursts on the bedstead when it seemed words failed him.

'It's not as though the Toymaker is short on resources,' said the Doctor, in between sentences. 'He doesn't need to save on building costs, so why does he build a high-tech barrier, when bricks and mortar would do fine?' He waved his hand at the once-existent walls and door to demonstrate his point. The Claw's response seemed to satisfy him, for he handed the antennae over, and watched fascinated as the terrible jaws closed over it as gentle as a summer's breeze. There being no reply to his rhetorical question, the Doctor supplied his own answer. 'Because that's what he knows, and that's what he controls the easiest.'

'You said he was telepathic,' pointed out Peri.

'Yeah, and summat else,' added Kevin, somewhat unhelpfully.

'Telekinetic,' supplied Peri.

'Yeah,' added Kevin, none the wiser.

'That's right,' encouraged the Doctor.

'So the barrier was made up from his mind?' speculated Peri.

The Doctor nodded at the seemingly empty doorway. 'I'm sure it is. But the inconvenience of having to sustain the mental effort bored him. He made it a simple electro-mechanical device which he could switch on and off with a flick of his mind.'

'If he's telepathic,' mused Kevin, reaching a conclusion with the speed of a glacier, 'he can hear everything we're thinking . . .'

'Only if he's listening all the time,' insisted the Doctor. 'Think of it yourself,' he invited, ever the optimist. 'If you could receive every thought of every person within say, what – five miles? You'd go mad. You'd have to discipline your mind absolutely to filter out the thoughts you don't want to hear. And you'd have to be able to turn them off altogether if you wanted to do some thinking yourself. I'm gambling that the Toymaker's "Great Work" is of much more interest to him than anything we might be chatting about down here.' He looked around him. '*Particularly* what we have been chatting about down here . . . Now I've been talking it over with my friend the Mechanic here, and he thinks it'll work. He'll need a hand, though. Rather literally, I'm afraid,' he added, looking at SB, who looked as cheerful and as mystified as ever. A voice stopped the conversation in its tracks.

'Doctor . . .'

The Doctor spun round to see Stefan standing in the doorway, his grin never more wolfish. 'Ah, ready to come out and play, are we?' he called, drily. He rose, dusted his trousers off and paused to fix Peri with the hardest stare he could muster.

'When you want me, just give me a yell, will you?' He continued to fix her with that stare as he repeated, 'Just give me a yell.'

Peri nodded, understandably bemused, and the Doctor, with a half cheery wave, turned and went through the door, obviously with the barrier lowered for that purpose. And obviously only for that purpose, for when Kevin started to follow him, he ran smack into it and was hurled back several feet.

The Doctor walked off down the corridor and, stopping only to stare at Peri, Stefan walked slowly after him.

The corridors and the entire complex seemed strangely silent to the Doctor as he walked along. Or maybe it was his sense of gloom and doom which he'd fought hard to disguise from the others in the eventually overcrowded prison cell. Given the state they were in, he thought, maybe the pink cloud had the right idea. It suddenly struck him that the last time he'd looked at the pink cloud, it could easily have been mistaken for an ostrich rather than a three-legged beastie, given that it had only two legs and its head was stuck in the sand . . .

'I understand you play backgammon,' he threw at Stefan.

'A little,' was the short reply.

'We must have a game sometime.'

'But there is no more time, Doctor. Not for you. Besides, I have played once tonight already.'

'Have you? Have you indeed?' answered the Doctor grimly. Stefan motioned him forward with his pistol, and the Doctor climbed the stairs before him.

The corridor at the top was of quite a different style. Once more echoes of the Orient could be detected, and the Doctor was not at all surprised when Stefan motioned him to a halt outside an ornate and deeply carved door, whilst Stefan reached across him and knocked respectfully. There was no reply the Doctor could hear, but Stefan turned the handle and motioned the Doctor through.

'Ah, Doctor,' greeted the Toymaker, 'good of you to come.' He rose from behind his desk in an elaborate gesture of courtesy.

'Your choice, Toymaker, not mine,' replied the Doctor shortly. 'I do admire your taste in furnishings, I must say, but don't you think that tapestry's a bit *too* recherché? I mean, I'm very flattered and all, but I did make it in a hurry, and the Han-Sen original was awfully grubby by the time it reached me.'

'During one of your usual meddlings, I take it?' asked the Toymaker, quite unfazed by the Doctor's claim.

'Not mine,' replied the Doctor, idly. 'As I recall, the British Fleet was busy shelling the city at the time. They were the ones doing the meddling.'

'The Opium Wars?'

118

'Yes. Right up your street, all that, wasn't it?'

'I wasn't there.'

'No, or I'm sure we would have met. With your interest in matters Eastern, the downfall of the Chinese Empire was a foregone conclusion anyway.'

'You do me too much honour . . .'

'Oh, I didn't mean to,' replied the Doctor, disingenuously, 'after all, you lost, didn't you? It would have suited you far more to keep the corrupt Empire going for another couple of thousand years. Lots of room for games in Imperial China, eh?'

'Lots of room for games anywhere on this planet, Doctor. As you, and I, have remarked, the human race is a very ingenious little species.'

'They can be more than ingenious if they're pointed in the right direction.'

'How very patronising.'

'That's another difference between you and me, Toymaker. I'd sooner patronise them than butcher them.'

The Mandarin sighed with regret. 'I am yet again astonished that with such differences between us, we can still enjoy the odd game together.'

'I don't enjoy them, odd or not. I play them because you force me to.'

'And you are confident of winning again this time?'

'Why not? You can't have got any better.'

'Whilst you have had lot of practice?'

'As much as I wanted.'

'Good. We shall see if you are sufficiently prepared . . .'

The Mandarin crossed to the door, and Stefan stepped forward to open it for him. The Doctor promptly sat in the chair before the desk and once again nonchalantly hooked his leg over the arm and casually swung it to and fro.

'Why did you come here, Toymaker,' he asked lightly. 'The natives *are* ingenious, we're agreed on that, but no more so than a dozen other places I could name in this galaxy alone.'

The Mandarin looked at him, long and hard. Then he crossed slowly to sit in his own chair behind the desk.

'But it's not just ingenuity, Doctor. The local inhabitants have an obsessive interest in games rivalling my own. In one of their greatest wars, one that was waged by the entire planet, they stopped fighting one day and played a game of football together – between the barbed wire, can you imagine? There's a tribe to the east who, until very recently, played a game using their fallen enemies' *heads* as a ball! My little pranks pale in comparison.'

'There are madmen and cruel children in every society –' began the Doctor, but the Toymaker leaned forward and cut him off.

'But not at *every* level of that society . . . No, Doctor, sometimes I think this world was *made* for me . . .' And he leaned back in his chair, relaxing, the glint back in his eye.

The Claw was tapping on his pipe, a disconsolate and wistful note to the clanging iron. There was no one there to understand a word he was saying.

'He can tap all he likes,' grunted Kevin. 'I don't know what he wants . . .'

'Don't understand how we can "give him a hand",' grumbled SB, 'if we can't –' He got no further with his complaint, for the Claw, in frustration or out of pique at being ignored it was difficult to say, had moved its attention from the pipe, scuttled over towards SB with surprising speed and agility, and had firmly and most convincingly snapped the serrated edge of his principal appendage around SB's arm, just above the elbow. The claw started to close, slowly.

'Here, steady on, old chap,' muttered SB. The grip tightened. SB's voice filled with alarm and anger. 'D'you mind? That's my second best arm!'

'That's it!' exclaimed Peri.

'Eh?' queried SB, trying without success to fight off the unwelcome amputation.

'That's what he wants –'

'Bit early for lunch, old girl,' protested SB.

'Look, he can't very well build anything with just that claw of his, can he? If he's a mechanic, he'd need a whole range of tools – how does he hold them?'

The mechanic had certainly suspended operations on SB's arm, and Peri took the chance to swallow hard and examine the claw more closely. 'There, see?' she exclaimed excitedly. 'Look, all sorts of grooves and sockets.' And indeed, the claw was well equipped indeed to take a vast selection of fittings in, over, under and on its surface.

'Isn't evolution somethin'?' breathed Kevin, to no one in particular.

SB, intensely proud of any thought he gave vent to which was unconnected to fighting or eating, and was therefore higher philosophy, protested weakly at this barefaced hijack of one of his prouder moments. 'That's what I said . . . sort of . . . I think that's what I meant, anyway . . .' Unable to sustain the concentration for a moment longer, he gave up. 'Oh, all right then, just give it a couple of turns,' he volunteered, grumpily, which was just as well as the mechanic seemed to be eyeing his head in a thoughtful manner, as if deciding to go right to the root of the problem.

Kevin gripped the arm just above the wrist and started to turn it, slowly. The wrong way, it seemed, for SB gave a yell, and Kevin muttered, 'All right, all right,

121

what d'you think I am, a neurosurgeon or summat?'
when the arm screwed off smoothly, leaving just a
multi-pin socket at the elbow. The mechanic eagerly
helped them fit it on the claw, where tiny grooves and
plates raised and lowered themselves until there was a
perfect fit.

'Actually,' murmured SB, interested in applied
mechanics for the first time in seven years, 'actually,
the trigger finger on that one's a bit stiff – you don't
think he could give it a bit of a tweak while he's at it,
do you?'

Peri looked at him coldly. '*You* ask him.'

SB gulped and smiled weakly as the Mechanic flexed
his new fingers with evident satisfaction.

The Doctor looked sharply at the Toymaker. 'The
vortex isn't running now, is it?'

'It fluctuates,' answered the Mandarin, disinterestedly.

'But you can intensify it?'

'On occasion . . .'

'It doesn't affect Stefan,' said the Doctor, almost to
himself.

'Doesn't it?' asked the Mandarin, a smile appearing
for the first time in several minutes.

'Nor any of the other people around you.'

'Like a child,' scoffed the Mandarin, 'fishing in a
dark pool.'

'I must say, you do seem to hang on to your staff for
an impressively long time – two hundred years for poor
old Shardlow, wasn't it?'

'I really couldn't say.'

'And how long has young Stefan been with you?'
'Young' Stefan gave him a look that would have
stunned a normal human being into a rigor of apology.

'Stefan was my first, and best, recruit,' answered the Toymaker fondly, nostalgia seeming to tug his mouth into the semblance of a smile. 'We had a game of dice, didn't we, Stefan, in Constantinople . . .'

Stefan also seemed to enjoy a trip down memory lane, for he to grinned broadly.

'We did, Lord. Never was I so pleased to lose a throw.' He turned to the Doctor, and announced with fierce pride, 'I was with Barbarossa. The Army of the Third Great Crusade against the Turk.'

'The Third Crusade, one long bloodbath. You killed more of each other than any enemy . . . One of the most savage and barbaric forces in history . . .' The Doctor's eyes narrowed in contempt.

'We took what we wanted,' sneered the henchman. 'We bowed our heads to our feudal Lord only. To no other man, of this world or any other.'

The Toymaker remembered a detail, something that had obviously been nagging him, like what colour shirt he'd been wearing, that sort of thing. 'You wagered a young Greek family, didn't you? They were Greek, weren't they?'

'They were, Lord,' grinned Stefan, 'strong, and good workers, too, given the right treatment.' He flexed his right wrist with his left hand to leave the Doctor in little doubt as to what the 'right treatment' was.

'Whatever became of them?' asked the Toymaker in evident concern.

'You sold them, Lord,' Stefan reminded him, shortly.

'I suppose I did,' mused the Mandarin, 'I mean, what else would I do with a Greek family? Oh, it's a long time ago . . .' With a wave of his hand, he consigned the Greek family, and the whole episode, to history.

'Eight hundred years,' breathed the Doctor.

'Does it seem a long time to wait, Doctor? For a game? I've been waiting a lot longer than that.'

'Time, as someone once said, is relative,' started the Doctor, and seemed set to go on into a detailed discussion of this fascinating subject, but the Toymaker would have none of it.

'Come, Doctor. Pleasant though our little chat is, we should move to a resolution of the main event, should we not?'

'I could simply refuse to play,' speculated the Doctor. 'What would you do then? Lock me away and throw away the key?'

'Something like that, Doctor, I imagine. And whilst you were locked away, Stefan here would have no end of amusing games of his own with your two companions . . . the young lady first, I would imagine . . .'

Stefan's grin lit the skies.

The Doctor jumped to his feet and strode towards the door. 'What are we waiting for, then?' he asked. 'Time's a-wasting . . .'

'And we mustn't waste time, must we, Doctor?' asked the Toymaker, softly. The Doctor looked at him closely. Had the Mandarin seen through him? How much did he know? *Had* he been listening and looking in at the wrong moment downstairs in the cell? The Toymaker's smile was as inscrutable as ever.

Peri was holding the antennae for the Mechanic, who was working on it deftly with SB's robotic arm attached to his claw. Close up, the alien wasn't nearly as repulsive as at a distance – a pleasant lemon scent came from the furry part of its body, and the mandibles either side of its mouth worked together to produce something akin to a tune – the monster's equivalent to whistling while it worked, she supposed.

'Back home, they've built an entire race of robots to do all the messy work,' SB was informing her. 'And funny thing is, those robots make the most marvellous after-dinner speakers – had one in our mess one time, jolly good, I must say . . . dunno how they do it . . .'

'Do what?' murmured Peri, against her better judgment.

'Well, you know, sort of teach them how to do that – speak well, crack the odd funny, you know . . . I mean you wouldn't think he'd know where to start, would you?' He gesticulated with his electronic stump at the monster, working away.

'No you wouldn't, would you?' answered Peri, softly. Was it her imagination, or was that hideous mouth with rows of teeth and vicious mandibles on either side actually smiling to itself?

'Wonder what the score is?' asked Kevin, of no one in particular.

Peri and SB looked at each other, wondering too . . .

Stefan watched carefully as the Doctor walked around the machine slowly, examining it in what seemed like some detail.

'It meets with your approval, I trust?' asked the Toymaker with the utmost courtesy.

The Doctor was pretty convinced that the question was a very idle one – if he said no, the Toymaker was hardly likely at this stage to say, 'Oh well, that's all right, old thing, let's just call the whole thing off . . .' The difficulty was not *thinking* about anything the slightest bit relevant to what was going on downstairs whilst he was in such close proximity to the Toymaker. He just didn't know how accurate the reports of his telepathic abilities were, or much of anything else about the man – being – thing – whatever it was . . .

'Fine,' he replied. 'I prefer the classic simplicity of Space Invaders myself. I mean, they were good for what, a good ten or fifteen seconds before they got boring.'

'I shall try to ensure you are not bored, Doctor,' promised the Toymaker, softly.

'I'm sure,' replied the Doctor, drily.

'There is only one rule –' the Toymaker began.

'You have to win, yes I know,' replied the Doctor absently. He was examining the screen, and noticed the All Time High Score sector. '125,550,' he read off. 'Who made that?'

'I did,' was the Toymaker's bland reply.

'And, of course, I have to take your word for that?' The Doctor smiled at him cynically.

'Don't you trust me, Doctor?' asked the Toymaker with wide-eyed innocence. The Doctor didn't bother to reply.

'Last player 175,' he read again. 'Poor chap . . .'

'Are you ready?' asked the Toymaker, archly.

'Not quite,' replied the Doctor, starting to roll up one of his jacket sleeves.

'Good,' replied the Toymaker calmly, as his hand reached forward and pressed the One Player button. The machine immediately sprang to life, and the Doctor's hands raced to the controls.

Chapter Nine

SB was propped against the bed, sitting on the floor.
He gassed on quite merrily as the Mechanic performed
what seemed to be open-heart surgery on him. Wires
and printed circuits and weird looking chips of this and
that protruded everywhere from a panel in his chest.
Occasionally, as the Mechanic tested another circuit,
SB's head would twitch, or his leg would move, or his
eyes would rotate like Catherine Wheels. Peri looked
on, at first in concern, then in simple bewilderment.

'Honestly,' chirped SB, 'doesn't hurt a bit . . . I
remember a terrific scrap off Vega V – that's what
we called it, but it wasn't really, just reminded us of
those wonderful old videoscans, where the good chaps
always wore the white space armour, d'you remember?
Oh, no, sorry, anyway, we were having a really terrific
time, dogfight all around the three moons, I just loved
it. Both arms, both legs and half me head gone, then
a lump of atomic shrapnel split my ship from stem to
stern, caught me in what was then me shoulder, just
about where your hand is now –' Peri moved her hand
hastily – 'did a marvellous job on me after that. Latest
everything, couldn't do enough. Wonderful thing,
medicine . . .'

The Mechanic worked on, unmoved.

'Very well paced, Toymaker. Almost enjoyable.'

The Doctor manipulated the controls which spoke
of countless hours misspending his youth in some
intergalactic dive or other, wherever Time Lords went

127

to misspend their youth, and, by the looks of things, at something considerably more demanding than Space Invaders . . . The monsters by the cars had been blown away a long time ago, and his score had already passed the 5000 mark. There was certainly no strain evident, not even a sign of any untoward concentration.

'Obviously a lot of research in this,' continued the Doctor, conversationally.

'Years and years,' smiled the Toymaker.

'At the funfair, I suppose?' There was only a look from the Toymaker in reply. 'All those bumps on grab-handles, pressure pads on the seats – whole place wired like an octopodal dishwasher. Random blood tests and medicals too, I shouldn't wonder.'

'I could hardly bring several million people in here for testing, could I?' asked the Toymaker, reasonably enough.

'And you would have to test millions to get these results, yes, I can quite see that,' agreed the Doctor in the same tone. 'But why? I mean, you don't need the money . . . do you?' The Toymaker smiled, and inclined his head self-deprecatingly. 'No, I can't see you in Debtors' Prison, worse luck. Oh they don't have those any more, do they? Not here anyway . . .' As the Doctor rattled on, the screen continued to explode in multi-coloured lights as he caught the monsters in his guns before they could catch him, but the pace was definitely hotting up. Better than 12,000 points now, halfway there and five lives up, with another bonus at 10,000, it seemed. 'Do I get my money back if I win?' he asked the Toymaker, blithely, but now keeping his eyes more on the screen. The Toymaker did not deign to answer, but merely watched the screen, inscrutably.

'So I said to the Sar'nt Major, "PF 4963" I said, "I know it's going to be hell, but I want that kite back in the air by 27.00 hours." And d'you know what he said to me . . . ?'

Peri shook her head, eyes drooping.

'He said, "Sir," he said "For you –" '

The rest of the reply was lost in a wailing squawk as the Mechanic moved the electronic hand in a snipping action to disconnect the android's voicebox. His lips continued to move, and his eyes moved from one to the other, Peri supposed in some form of protest at not being able to finish his interminable story. She soothed him as best she could.

'It's all right "old chap",' she said, 'I think he just needs your speaker for something . . .' She turned away to find one of the Mechanic's eyes moving on its stalk, examining her speculatively. She moved further away.

'I need all my bits and pieces myself,' she said, nervously. The Mechanic did not look convinced.

The atmosphere in the data room had changed perceptibly. There was a sheen of perspiration on the Doctor's forehead, and the noise from the machine was never-ending. Stefan had edged closer, but the Mandarin looked on, unchanged and unchanging.

The Doctor was fighting for his life now, the monsters on the screen coming from every direction, and now from the upper storeys of the buildings, too. The *crunchcrunchcrunch* noise had been taken over long ago, and added to by monsters of a different colour and size. They seemed more mobile now, more flexible, less monolithic and less unwieldy. Bending all his concentration to the task, the Doctor started to free himself.

He sent the front part of his mind forward, and, an inch at a time, further still, to meet the forces on the screen. Forward, forward, until that part of his mind was *in* the screen, amongst the buildings and the ruins

129

and the burnt out shells. He could sense the broken glass under foot and smell the burning rubber, hot plastic, hot metal of the firefight. The monsters came from all directions now, as if called by his presence, called to attack the intruder. His weaponry was burning white-hot, red and yellow lines of tracer arcing towards each threat as it appeared, sometimes before it appeared.

He ducked into a doorway, turning as he went to spray a window high on his left, blowing a sniper to pieces. Half-rolling his body, he hurtled out again as another shape drew a bead on him from inside the building. Firing from the hip, he blazed off down the street, screams of agony and hoarse yells of frustration following him, echoing down the deadly canyons of the city streets.

Unseen by him, the score counter spun dizzily, beyond 100,000 beyond 110,000, beyond 115,000 . . .

There was a stunning blow to his side, and another and another. He turned and fired blindly, and again, and the shells stopped exploding around him long enough for him to be able to take the next corner where, before he had time to recover, another of the monsters was firing at him. He moved back and felt the approach of more of them there, around the corner, then he roared out again, guns blazing, but another hit and another threw his aim off and ammunition was running low . . .

The Toymaker looked on, though with a faint smile creasing his mouth now, as he saw the two extra Lives vanish, snuffed out like tiny candles. And his eyes glinted.

Peri watched, fascinated, as the Mechanic delicately twisted and moulded together the antennae and the scrap from SB, fashioning what could only be a helmet of some sort. Even Kevin's attention was engaged, and poor old SB could only look and wonder. The Mechanic reached out and gently took Peri's arm, in just the same way as it had once taken the android's . . .

'Oh no,' protested Peri, 'you're not having *my* arm!' But the fingers of the electronic arm tightened insistently . . .

The counter moved again, not spinning frantically now, but turning through treacle, past 125,000 and towards the Toymaker's High Score. Stefan looked on aghast. Not a muscle moved on the Toymaker's face.

The streets were littered now with broken monsters, cracks starting to appear in the asphalt where the firefight had proved too much for the substance to stay stable. The cracks widened as the very ground rumbled. The frantic pitch of battle had slowed also, the steady *crunchcrunchcrunch* now returning to dominate the scene. The Doctor, exhausted, looked around for the source of the noise. There was something . . . something his other brain was telling him, something washed in or washed out by the fighting, by the insight he had into the mind that devised the game. The score hardly mattered. He knew he had only one life left and he had to find the answer before that was gone. Had to stay alive and find the answer . . . had to fight on . . . had to fight on . . .

The street filled with screaming crushing monsters one after the other as he blazed away, using the weaponry he had left as a hosepipe more than a precision piece. One life left and he was called back, called by the blare of electronic trumpets as the High Score was swept away. One more, two more, three bursts and again the street was clear before him . . . One life left. Still one life . . . One that was the answer . . . one . . . one alone . . .

He turned from the machine, sweat pouring from him, scars that would never show criss-crossing his mind.

'You're alone,' he croaked hoarsely at the Toymaker. 'One. One alone. There's just you, no one like you. Ever. This game – an empty city, a ghost city. And one, just one fighter, one enemy, one on his own . . . You're not from this Universe, are you?' He turned and walked towards the Toymaker, past the speechless Stefan, who had just witnessed, for the first time in eight hundred years another being's victory over his Lord and at one of his Lord's own games!

'The Game,' stammered the Mandarin, 'you're not thinking about the Game!'

There was a blare from the machine as the Doctor's last life was lost. The counter had come to a stop. 131,000, and the Toymaker's score was languishing under 'Last Player'. The Doctor appeared not to notice.

'You're not from this Universe,' he repeated, 'that's why there's no trace. That's why the Laws of this Universe don't concern you. You're from another Time and Space!'

The Mechanic, far from wanting to dissect Peri, had pulled her gently down to kneel on the floor, where he could help her better. The claw-arm now held the newly fashioned helmet, and he motioned for her to put it on.

'Sooner you than me,' muttered Kevin, as the headgear, resembling a cycling helmet with loose wires and pads dangling, was lowered gently onto her head. The Mechanic began delicately to adjust the fit, and to lead what appeared to be pressure-contact points to very specific and seemingly critical parts of her head. As he wove the wires carefully, a network started to take shape, almost hiding her features from view.

★

The Doctor was in full flow as the ramifications of his theory crashed in on him. Behind him, the game machine's ominous *crunchcrunchcrunch* had started distantly in the background. No one took any notice of it. Not yet . . .

'Whatever catastrophe it was,' the Doctor continued, as much to himself as to anyone else, 'it hurled you from your own universe into this one. You carry your own matter with you – you'd have to – not anti-matter, of course, otherwise you'd have started the next Big Bang – but different from ours.' He paused, thunderstruck by his own conclusions. 'Relativity,' he breathed, 'follow it through . . .' He swung round on the Toymaker again, 'Your own universe is receding from this one so fast, it's pushing your time back as it goes!' He stared at the Toymaker, awestuck. 'You'll live for millions of years!'

The Toymaker had a look of crushing despair on his face as he croaked out, 'I *have* done . . .'

The *crunchcrunchcrunch* was getting louder. A figure had appeared at the centre of the screen, and was growing larger, growing closer . . .

'The isolation of aeons,' whispered the Doctor, overcome with compassion for the being he'd detested all his adult life. 'The crushing loneliness of thousands of millenia . . . you poor, poor creature . . .'

Peri held the cap on her head with both hands, which had been carefully placed there by the Mechanic, who waited patiently as Kevin plugged the lead into the power point. A power hum started, which grew rapidly until it was difficult to hear anything else over it. The Mechanic moved not at all, waiting patiently for the next phase, for these weird and horrid creatures to play their part. Peri looked wildly from Kevin to the monster and to SB and back to the monster.

'Well, come on,' she called, 'what do I do now?' The power hum continued growing until it reached a pain threshold. Kevin held his hands over his ears and rolled on the floor, unable to bear it any longer. SB mouthed silently, unable to move or help, even if he knew how.

'I don't know what to do!' screamed Peri, though it was impossible to make herself heard over the noise, and impossible to tell if the Mechanic understood a word she was saying, 'Tell me what to do!'

The Toymaker's eye was cast on a far, far distant horizon, lost in a world vanished aeons ago.

'. . . and then I grew tired of even creating . . . ships, cities, continents, whole planets even. I transported life. I colonised, I helped it survive and thrive for millenia, hundreds of millenia, thousands . . .' His voice trailed off as he remembered, as the bitterness and the loneliness overcame him. He rounded on the Doctor, his eyes turning away from the softness of remembrance to the fury of the present. 'Until I came to destroy, wantonly, wilfully, the same ships, the same planets I'd helped to create, and that too became too easy and too empty . . . meaningless destruction is as appetising as meaningless creation and just as unfulfilling . . . Until I found distraction in the world of games, until I could throw off the pretence of purpose and meaning, until I too could be a prey to chance and hazard . . .'

The glint was back in his eye now, more dangerous than ever before as it merged with the gleam of triumph. The Doctor, seeing the difference, whirled round to see the formation of the monster on the screen, to see it grow larger and larger until the screen could not contain it. The *crunchcrunchcrunch* had reached its inevitable crescendo, and the electronic monster stood outside the machine, brighter, if anything, and more terrible than before. The Toymaker's triumph screeched out at last.

'A hazard, Doctor, which you have lost!'

The monster turned and lumbered slowly towards the transfixed Time Lord.

Peri had draggged a reluctant Kevin to her and yelled in his ear, 'Is there a button? A switch? Anything?'

'Nothing I can see,' he yelled back.

The Mechanic seemed to go into a frantic wardance of its own, rattling, gesticulating clattering and tapping with whatever came to hand – or claw. In an anguished voice, Peri could only repeat helplessly, 'What am I supposed to *do*?'

The Doctor, staring at the monster, backed away slowly. His face bore the full horror of what he was seeing – not the monster, for he had seen much much more repellent examples than that, and the worst examples were always manmade, but the purpose behind the monster . . .

'Kill him!' screamed the Toymaker. 'KILL HIM!'

Peri's eyes were wide open, wide as they could go. Kevin lay dazed on the floor where a casual by-blow from the Mechanic's claw had thrown him, the same claw that was now fastening itself relentlessy around Peri's throat . . .

'Doctor!' she cried. 'Doctor!' She tried in vain to force the closing pincers apart. The monster's bulbous veined eyes were scant inches from hers, an unfeeling, deadly purpose behind them. At the very top of her voice she screamed with all her might, 'DOCTOR!'

The Toymaker staggered, his hands to his head, his face screwed up in pain and confusion. Stefan had come out of his trance and was back to doing what he was best at – protecting his Lord. Gun in hand, he was circling slowly to keep away from the electronic giant and reach a point where he had a clear shot at the Doctor. He turned his head in agitation at the obvious discomfort of his master. Even the Monster seemed confused, distracted, as though it had lost its bearings on its target. It lumbered round half a step to advance on Stefan, but with the agile step sideways of a practised swordsman, Stefan skirted it neatly and was about to swing on the Doctor when the Doctor took matters into his own hands – literally. Grabbing Stefan's gun-hand in both of his own, he pivoted sharply and swung the henchman bodily round in a full circle. Already off-balance, Stefan's momentum carried him forward, and it was all he could do to keep his feet. At the end of the circle, the Doctor, gauging the trajectory as well as he could, released the hand, and Stefan went tumbling, smack up against the Monster . . .

There was a short scream of pain – and another, this time of fear – and the monster's hands did the rest. Stefan slumped, smouldering, to the ground.

Peri's scream was echoing and reverberating around the room, as if hitting a giant acoustic mirror, distorting, building, building, wavering wildly and crashing back like a wave on the Toymaker, who staggered still, his hands over his ears, unable to block out even a tiny part of the noise. His contorted face seemed about to burst as he tried to stop the dreadful falling tower of sound as, with a *whump* he crashed into the Monster. Turning around, eyes staring wider if that were possible, he watched helplessly as the Monster raised its hands and placed them on either side of the Toymaker's head. Peri's screaming was wiped out by the intensity of the power-hum which followed, and, as the Toymaker slumped to the floor, the Monster started to fade and disappear from sight . . .

The Doctor took only a split second to glance at the fallen Mandarin and, without any further hesitation, raced from the room, down towards the prison cell and Peri.

The door barrier was down, and the Mechanic was already switching off his machine, by the simple expedient of snipping through the power cable with his claw. He looked vaguely gratified at the sparks as the circuit shorted, and by then the Doctor was in, striding over to Peri and helping her remove the helmet from her head.

'Well done!' he called over to the Mechanic, who, either by coincidence or through a deeper understanding than he'd let on before, waved a claw in friendly acknowledgement.

'What about me?' protested Peri, feebly.

'Yeah, an' me,' groaned Kevin, fairly sure this was the sort of thing the Lord Mayor gave banquets for.

'Don't worry,' replied the Doctor, deliberately misunderstanding, 'you'll be fine. Now come *on* . . .' and with that he was off again, tearing out of the door and up the stairs again. Not out through the tunnels to freedom, but back into the Wolf's Lair . . .

'Search everywhere you can think of,' called the Doctor as he burst into the Toymaker's study, and started looking himself in the drawers of the giant carved desk.

'For what?' asked Peri, ever a stickler for detail.

'His tele-mechanical relay,' replied the Doctor, exasperated that he should have to fill in every little detail.

'His tele-what?' queried Kevin, who rather fancied himself well up on the high-tech scene.

'Tele-mechanical relay,' repeated the Doctor, as if trying to win an argument against a particularly stubborn opponent. He abandoned his search of the desk and crossed swiftly to the video-screen, feeling round the edges for an opening. 'The relay he uses to operate the holo-field downstairs – and for everything else he wants to control without really trying.'

Instinctively, Peri looked around, trying to spot it. 'What does it look like?' she remembered to ask.

'Haven't the faintest idea,' replied the Doctor. 'Just look for something you've ever seen before and can't imagine a use for and we'll start with that.' With uncharacteristic vandalism, he took hold of the bottom edge of one of the wall-coverings, and ripped it from its fixings.

'Over on that other wall!' he cried. 'Rip it down! It must be here somewhere, and we've got to find it before he regains consciousness . . .'

The Toymaker's fingers, stretched out on the floor, flexed and stirred. His arm slowly pulled in as he levered himself up groggily to look at the barren data room. The only inhabitant apart from himself was Stefan, and the Mandarin painfully pulled himself over to where he lay. With an effort he turned his faithful henchman over and, with a final heave, Stefan flopped over on his back, obviously not merely unconscious. But then, the Toymaker had never intended the electronic monster to merely stun anyone. As he registered the fact, the Toymaker's face darkened again.

'Doctor . . .' he whispered.

The Doctor spun his head as he heard the dreaded voice once again. His efforts took on a frantic haste as he turned back to the wall beneath the tapestry the Toymaker had expressed such interest in during his previous visit to the room. With a cry of triumph, he tore it from the wall, reaching behind a control panel to force it away from its fixings. Behind was a metal cylinder, about a foot long and two inches in diameter, with wires springing from terminals at both ends.

'Doctor . . .' the voice began, booming now instead of whispering, dwarfing the effect Peri's screams had had, crashing around the room and shattering without discrimination the video-screen and a priceless Ming vase next to it. Screwing up his face and tucking his head into his shoulders as if against a hurricane force wind, the Doctor yanked the wires from one end of the cylinder.

'DOC –'

The voice had the force of an exploding shell, and the silence was the more shocking as the Doctor yanked the wires from the other end of the tube. He, then Peri and finally even Kevin breathed a sigh of relief as the thunder died away.

'Come on,' said the Doctor grimly, 'no more games.' And with that he led the way swiftly out of the room.

The Toymaker had abandoned his keening over the fallen Stefan and, as the trio came into the room, he was rising to his feet. The Doctor motioned the other two to stay just where they were as he moved towards the Toymaker.

'I have had millions of years to devise a punishment for you,' hissed the Toymaker, 'I have millions more to inflict it.' He raised himself threateningly to his full height.

'Time you have, yes, Toymaker, time enough to drive any being mad. But you're no more a threat to anyone . . .' With that, he raised the cylinder in one hand and gave a sharp twist to one end. There was an audible click as something locked, and the Toymaker started forward. He stopped, abruptly, slamming into an obstruction. An invisible obstruction. The Doctor held up the cylinder.

'Your own telepathic relay switch for the holo-field which now surrounds you. Tuned to your own thought frequency. Locked into a loop by the power of your own brain. It will function as long as your brain functions, even when you are asleep. Until you're dead.' With what seemed like overwhelming fatigue, the Time Lord turned, and started for the door, Peri and Kevin preceding him.

The Toymaker's face grew longer, his eyes staring as the enormity of his fate dawned upon him. His mouth opened and moved in what must have been a tearing scream . . . a timeless scream . . . a scream for all eternity . . . The Doctor turned back for one last look, a bleak and immovable sadness in his eyes.

'I detest caging even the wildest beast, Toymaker,' he announced, flatly, unsure even if the Mandarin could hear him, 'but for you there is no other answer . . . Goodbye . . .' He turned and left the room without another backward glance.

In the confines of his cell, the Toymaker began to desperately explore the tiny limits of his invisible, eternal prison.

In the corridor outside, Peri voiced the anxious question, 'Is he unconscious again?'

'Unfortunately for him, no,' replied the Doctor.

'We'd better get out quick, then,' muttered Kevin.

'He can't hurt you now,' the Doctor said gloomily. 'He's locked in the same sort of holo-field as he kept us in downstairs, powered by his own thoughts, locked in an eternal, endless loop.' He hefted the cylinder in his hand.

'His telepathy!' Peri exclaimed. 'He can order someone outside to destroy the relay.' Kevin looked nervously at the cylinder, and just as nervously at his companions. Fortunately for the Doctor, Peri had provided a point

140

upon which he could vent his feelings. He turned on the poor girl savagely.

'You know nothing about time, Peri. Nothing. I've just told you – he's trapped in an endless loop. The eternal circle. No beginning, no end. The Law which applies to all Universes. His thoughts will just go round and round, trapping him, holding him, echoing all around him for the rest of time . . . it's . . . loath- some . . .' he sagged against the wall, overcome by the dreadful fate he'd condemned the Toymaker to, a fate which the Doctor, the Time Lord, could appreciate only too well. Peri touched his arm gently.

'When I screamed, I saw a bright picture in my head – a picture of a burning giant, a monster, an unstoppable monster. Wouldn't *that* have gone on forever too?'

'When you screamed, you flooded his mind,' ex- plained the Doctor almost absently. 'The Mechanic rigged up a mental broadcast transmitter on the same wavelength as the holo-field he used for our prison – it reversed the flow of his thoughts for a split second, and you must have caught the backwash.'

'And the monster I saw would have rampaged over the whole Earth?'

'It certainly would. That and thousands like it, all generated by anyone losing at the Toymaker's latest game. That was his Great Work,' he finished, bitterly.

'Then you had no choice,' she said, gently.

'But don't you see, Peri? I know exactly what it would be like, the endless unbroken stream of time . . . nothing but time . . .' The Time Lord seemed to sink into melancholia, into his own cosmic angst.

Peri decided a practical problem needed a practical solution. 'Well,' she started, brightly, 'we can't just leave him where he is, cluttering up Blackpool for the rest of eternity. We'll get back to the TARDIS and you can use the transdimensional stabilizer to whisk him

141

off to somewhere he won't be noticed. Then you can ferry our friends downstairs back to where they came from.'

'What d'you think I am,' he spluttered, 'a cosmic taxi service?'

Before she could form a suitable reply, the breath caught in her throat. Along the gloomy corridor a figure shambled towards them, not quite humanoid, not quite alien, its face seemingly composed of a single, gaping, cavernous hole.

'There's a helluva racket goin' on,' the figure yawned. 'I'm trying to get some kip in –'

'Geoff!' exclaimed Kevin.

'Hello, Kev,' said the missing brother amiably. 'What are you doing here? D'you know the time?' By way of a reply, Kevin caught him in a gigantic bear-hug, which, from the look on Geoff's face, was not the usual reaction he provoked in his elder brother.

'Shall we leave Romulus and Remus to sort things out?' muttered the Doctor to Peri. She nodded her agreement, and they both made their way to the door at the far end of the corridor.

'Kevin,' he called back as he was about to go through the door, 'somewhere in here you'll find the patents for all those machines – except one, that is – they're yours as much as anyone's. Should be worth quite a bit of money. Why don't you use it to close down the Toymaker's factory? The term "takeover" seems very apt under the circumstances . . .'

'I've always fancied setting up on me own, like,' replied Kevin, suddenly transformed into a pillar of the commercial establishment.

'Take my tip,' grinned the Doctor, 'always start at the top if you can.'

'Ta,' said Kevin, 'See you –' But the Doctor and his companion were gone.

'You know,' said Geoff to his brother, confidentially, 'in the couple of days I've been here, I've seen more oddballs –'

'Coupla days?' asked Kevin.

'Yeah.' Geoff continued in the same confidential tone of voice. 'You get so you don't ask any daft questions, Kev. Know what I mean?'

The Doctor, the spring back in his step, strode down the corridor, Peri struggling to keep up. He made straight for a door off to the right, half hidden by a curtain. Peri stopped at another corridor leading off the the left.

'Where are you going?' she called. 'This is the way out.'

The mischievous gleam in his eye matched the smile as he replied, 'But this is the way back to the funfair . . . coming?'

Peri hesitated for only a moment and then, with a grin, hurried after him.

ARE YOU BUYING DOCTOR WHO MAGAZINE?

Every monthly issue of *Doctor Who Magazine* is packed with information about the world's longest running SF television programme, including news, interviews, archives, and a brand new comic strip featuring the current Doctor! Special reports cover subjects such as visual effects, design, merchandise and reviews of all the new Target Books.

Subscribe to *Doctor Who Magazine* by filling out or copying the coupon below, enclosing a cheque for the appropriate amount (made payable to Marvel Comics Ltd.), to *Doctor Who Magazine* Subscriptions, P.O. Box 500, Leicester LE99 0AA.

Subscription rates as follows: United Kingdom £15.00; Overseas £25.00; US $45.00. Offer expires September 30th 1989; please allow 28 days for your subscription to take effect.